DREAM SPINNER

DREAM SPINNER

BONNIE DOBKIN

flux
TM
Woodbury, Minnesota

First Edition
First Printing, 2006

Book design by Steffani Chambers
Cover design and illustration by Kevin R. Brown
Cover tapestry image © Photodisc
Editing by Rhiannon Ross

Flux, an imprint of Llewellyn Publications

Library of Congress Cataloging-in-Publication Data (pending)
ISBN 13: 978-0-7387-0919-2
ISBN 10: 0-7387-0919-0

Flux
A Division of Llewellyn Worldwide, Ltd.
2143 Wooddale Drive, Dept. 0-7387-0919-0
Woodbury, MN 55125-2989, U.S.A.
www.fluxnow.com

Printed in the United States of America

To the men in my life—
Kevin, Michael, Bryan,
and Jeff, my wonderful Bear.

And for my parents.

Acknowledgements

Thanks to everyone who pushed and prodded, encouraged and applauded:

My wonderful agent, Erin Murphy, who took a chance on a stray from Chicago.

To all the folks at Flux—Andrew, Rhiannon, Steffani, and Kevin—who turned a bunch of pages into a book.

My nieces and nephews, who also happen to be my biggest fans—Ethan, Morgan, Eli, Spencer, Adam, Stacey, Alex, and Samantha.

My brothers, Allen and Phil—just because I love them—and my "sisters," Laura, Kim, and Beth.

My first critics, Alex King and Stephanie Axelson, and their teacher, Gary Puhy.

Iya Ta'Shia and the Mad House gang, for getting me back to work.

June, for peace of mind as I juggled my life, and the Group, for always being there.

Margaret K. McElderry and Robert Brown, for wisdom along the way.

And Jori B., for the name.

PROLOGUE

The old house crouched in the overgrown lot as though it was ashamed to be seen. Warped shingles clung to its sunken roof, and paint curled off the scarred, graying walls. On the second floor, blackened windows stared at the ruins of a long-dead garden.

A shadow moved behind one of those windows.

A dark man with burning eyes leaned against the sill, watching hungrily as long, late-afternoon shadows crept across the flattened grass and smothered the last bits of daylight.

"It will be dark soon," he murmured, his tongue flicking across his lips. He raised his voice slightly. "Everything is ready, I presume."

There was a small sound of reassurance. A smile twisted across the dark man's face, and he looked once more out of the window.

"Come," he whispered. "I am waiting."

ONE
DETOUR

The black eye hadn't been nearly enough, Jori thought. She should have knocked Marisa flat and yanked out every strand of her long hair, handful by handful. Or removed her new jeweled navel ring—the hard way. Or maybe, she thought, absently fingering the web of scars on her right arm, maybe she could have hired one of the school troglodytes to lock her in a forgotten dumpster for a day or so, just long enough for rats to nibble her into insanity.

Jori smiled slightly, adding that image to the chamber of horrors she was designing for Marisa's exclusive use. The chamber was becoming pretty elaborate after so many months of planning. But then, nothing was too good for her former best friend.

Too bad the thing would never be operational. As it was, Marisa was already able to mask the bruise under her eye with just a light dab of makeup. And her adoring group of hangers-on were making a huge fuss over their wounded leader, fighting over who would fetch lunch for her in the cafeteria or have the honor of lugging her backpack through the halls. Jori, on the other hand, was still suffering through a ten-day detention. And this was only day six.

Unfair. Totally, hideously unfair.

She jumped as someone tugged at her sleeve.

"Psst . . . Jori."

"Go away."

Newt McAllister, resident geek, had folded his long body into the aisle next to her. He was peering anxiously toward the scarred metal desk at the front of the room, the guard tower from which balding Mr. Alvarez ruled over the detention hall. The little man appeared to be in a coma—his eyes were half-closed, his head tilted back.

"Okay," Newt whispered. "Time to bust out of here. Jori. You with me?"

"Newt, do me a favor and climb back in your tree with the rest of the squirrels."

"Good! That's good. Better if Alvarez doesn't think we're in this thing together. Okay, here's the plan. In exactly four minutes, you create a distraction. Start moaning, maybe, or have some kind of convulsion. Got it?"

"Sure."

"When Alvarez comes to see what's wrong, I'll wrestle him to the ground, and you can make your escape." His eyes became tragic. "As for me . . . if I die, I die."

Well, at least he's consistent, Jori thought. From what she'd heard, Newt had a little problem with reality. In fact, his detention was the result of his freeing all the rats in the biology lab, then leaping onto a table while shouting "Freedom!" at the top of his lungs. There had been close to a thousand dollars worth of damage as his classmates scrambled onto counters and chairs to avoid the liberated rodents.

And now this savior of mice was crouching next to her, planning their escape from Room 154.

"My only regret," Newt continued, looking at her mournfully through his long, dirty-blond hair, "is that I will never know *you*, my dear. Never explore the wonders of your mind, never touch your soft—"

"You touch anything and I'll break your face."

It was now 4:26 on what felt like the longest day she had spent in this room so far. And the way she saw it, she didn't deserve to be here at all. Yes, maybe a couple of her punches had connected with Marisa's face. But not before Marisa had delivered the real knock-out blows.

Staring blankly at Mr. Alvarez, Jori replayed in her mind the conversation that had sparked her fury. She had just brushed by Marisa and one of her little freshman acolytes, a twig-like girl hoping to enter her idol's inner circle.

"God, who's that?" the girl gasped, staring after Jori.

"No one important."

"But what's with her face? And her arm?"

"Car accident. Her and her dad. She got sliced and diced by the glass."

"Jeez. And what happened to him?"

Marisa shrugged. "Road kill."

The last bell finally rang. Grabbing her backpack, Jori bolted from the classroom and out of the school. Just outside the entrance, though, she paused and peered up into one corner of the doorway. She smiled, the tension draining from her.

The web was even bigger today, capturing the soft glow of the entry lights in its delicate stands. Its owner—a large, almost colorless spider that Jori had first noticed several days before—sat motionless in the shadows, waiting patiently for its next meal to wander into its net.

"Congratulations," Jori said softly. "It looks really great."

"Who are you talking to?"

It was Newt. Jori flushed, her face almost matching her short red hair.

"No one. Nothing." She paused. " A spider."

"A spider."

"Yeah."

"Huh," he said, addressing the inhabitant of the web. "And people say I'm weird."

Jori glared at him, then hitched her backpack higher on her shoulders and ran down the steps. Newt hurried after her.

"Jori, wait. I was kidding. You're not weird."

She kept walking. "I know I'm not. Just ugly. An ugly girl who happens to like bugs."

"You're not ugly. As for your attraction to creepy-crawlies . . ." He paused. "Well, that just means you probably could learn to like other strange and unusual things. Like salamanders. Or Newts."

"Don't hold your breath."

She took longer strides, trying to put as much distance between herself and Newt as possible. But his footsteps continued behind her. After a minute, she whipped around.

"Exactly *what* is your problem?"

Startled, Newt scrambled backwards, tripping over his own feet. He fell into a pile of leaves—leaves that had been masking a puddle of mud.

"Ugh." He looked up sheepishly, then reached out one hand. "Please, m'lady," he said. "Wouldst thou help a poor knave who hast fallen for thee?"

Jori folded her arms.

"Right." He sighed, struggled to his feet, and began wiping the sludge from his clothes. Jori looked at him critically. Newt was very tall and very thin, a scarecrow of a boy with a wide mouth, a narrow nose, and a long neck punctuated by an oversized Adam's apple. He wore threadbare denims and a tattered olive jacket that looked like it had come from an army surplus shop. His shaggy hair fell halfway to his shoulders.

"Well?" Jori asked. "Why are you following me? You training to be a stalker or something?"

"I was following you," Newt said, peeling off the last black leaves, "because of daylight saving time."

"What are you talking about?"

"Daylight saving. It started Sunday. So it's the first time it's been dark in the afternoon since we've been imprisoned. I just thought you might want some company walking home."

Jori didn't reply. This wasn't the answer she'd been expecting. And, she had to admit, she'd never been very comfortable walking home at night. Too many dark figures slumped in alleys or eyeing her from doorways. In fact, that was one of the things everyone at school had whispered about after her sister . . . *Stop it,* she told herself. She looked defiantly at Newt.

"Don't bother. I can take care of myself."

"No one said you couldn't. Anyhow, it's not a bother." He waited. "Well?"

"Suit yourself."

She continued walking, Newt by her side, his gangly body dipping slightly with every step. After a few minutes, Jori grew uncomfortable, worried that Newt might suddenly decide to attack a lamppost or talk to a hydrant.

"You don't have to do this," she underscored. "Won't someone be wondering where you are?"

He shook his head. "My dad's out late most nights, and he travels a lot. One of those financial robber barons you read about. Lives to pillage and plunder and destroy small businesses."

"What about your mom?"

"She disappeared years ago. Something she married disagreed with her."

"Sorry," Jori mumbled.

He shrugged. "So anyhow, the only ones waiting for me are Braveheart, Aragorn, and what's-her-name—Ripley—from those old *Alien* movies." Jori raised an eyebrow, and Newt grinned. "I watch a lot of old movies. They pass the time. And they . . . kind of get me away from things for a while, you know?"

"From what?"

"Everything."

Jori processed this information. Okay, so Newt's life sucked, too. And at school, he was tortured almost as much as she was. Only in his case, the torture involved the words "freak" and "gay." So maybe she could be civil.

"I do the same thing. Escape, I mean. But with me, it's books."

"Books. You mean those things with covers, and letters on the front, and lots of paper inside?"

"Yeah, those."

"Wow. Didn't know anyone used 'em anymore."

Jori attempted a smile.

"So where do you live?" she asked. "I've never seen you come this way."

"Yeah. That's because our place is in Uptown. The robber baron has to keep up appearances, you know." He stretched out his arms, displaying his motley outfit to full effect. "I make him crazy."

Jori jerked to a stop, her flash of goodwill gone. The guy had serious money. At least, his dad did. And, Uptown—a pricey neighborhood of recently "gentrified" buildings—was in exactly the opposite direction from her own neighborhood. Newt was adding nearly an hour to his trip home.

"Okay," she said, "what's going on?"

"What are you talking about?"

"Why are you walking me home? You slumming? Or trying to prove something to all the goons at school? Think that just because I have a face from a slasher movie, you'll have it easy?"

Newt stared at her. "No. I don't. And your face isn't—" He hesitated. "It's just that . . . well, you've had it kind of tough lately. And I thought maybe you could use a friend."

He feels sorry for me, she realized, her jaw tightening. *He* feels sorry for *me!*

"Listen, don't do me any favors. And if I ever decide I do need a friend, I'll look for someone a lot more impressive than the Lord of the Rats."

Newt flinched. But then his eyes, normally a soft, lazy blue, turned hard as slate. "Hey, I don't need this. You don't want me around? No problem. I'm leaving."

"Fine."

"Fine."

They stormed off in opposite directions.

★   ★   ★

Jori stalked away under the flat, yellow glow of the streetlights, swearing with every step. Her mood deteriorated even further when she turned onto Bridgeview and saw the sidewalks and streets ripped up, blocked by orange-striped barriers and blinking amber lights.

"Perfect," she muttered, then spotted a detour sign pointing toward a narrow sidestreet. She headed toward it, then refocused her anger on Newt. Who did that jerk think he was, anyway? Thinking she needed help from him. Thinking she'd even *want* a friend like him. Where'd he get the nerve to . . .

To what?

Be friendly?

She chewed on her lip, troubled. So the guy had been nice. Big crime. The problem was, she wasn't used to nice anymore. She was used to just the opposite—averted eyes and ugly remarks, dating from the moment she returned from the hospital. Her first painful lessons in just how cruel people can be.

And things had only gotten worse when her sister Lisa disappeared. Jori could still still feel the stares burning across her back, hear the cobra's nest of whispers following her through the hallways.

That her?

Yeah. Family's cursed, dude. First the dad. Now the sister.

Think she's still alive?

Not after all these weeks. Not around here.

Marisa, of course, had carefully tended to this little firestorm of gossip, further isolating the person she had once called her best friend. She fanned the fears of those who were repulsed by Jori's injuries, and fed the swirling rumors surrounding Lisa's disappearance. Remembering this, Jori felt her throat tighten. Why had Marisa turned on her, just when Jori had needed her most?

She shook her head, angry with herself for even caring anymore. She glanced up to get her bearings, and her steps slowed. Somehow, she had wandered into the maze of narrow alleyways that snaked off from the main avenue. She felt a twinge of fear. It wasn't like her to space out that badly.

She crept forward, jumping at every small sound. Dark buildings brooded on either side, and ancient street lamps grinned at her, their broken bulbs glinting like teeth. Jori had no idea which direction to head in, and there was no one around to ask. No one, that is, that she could see.

A sharp clicking broke the silence. It was regular, measured, followed by the rustle of something creeping through dead leaves.

Click-click. Ssshhhh. Click. Ssshhhhh.

Sweat prickled on Jori's arms. Footsteps, she thought. Following me.

Click. Sssshhhh. Click-click. Ssshhhh.

No, not footsteps. At least not human ones. Jori's imagination took over, drawing hideous pictures in harsh, black lines. Pictures of something monstrous, something deformed. Something that waited hungrily for anyone stupid enough to get lost in this web.

And it was getting closer.

Jori ran, but the alley closed in around her, a perverse obstacle course. She jumped across potholes, stumbled over bricks, and sidestepped an abandoned couch that lay in her path like a gutted cow. Then she tripped over a metal pipe, falling against the pitted walls of an old building and scraping the skin from her hands.

She barely paused as pain shot through her. *Faster,* she thought. *I have to go faster.* She lurched forward, yanking at the straps of her overloaded backpack and letting it drop to the ground.

Now a new sound began to fight with her own terrified gasps. A low, fierce growl, growing louder and angrier.

Jori moaned, frantically racing around corners until she could have been heading back into the claws of whatever was hunting her. Sobs tore from her chest, and she shot frightened glances over her shoulder.

"Help me!" she shrieked. "Somebody help me!"

A black shape leaped from the looming darkness, and Jori screamed.

It was a dog.

Huge and barrel-chested, the animal stared at her with ice-blue eyes, its open mouth a cavern of sharp teeth. Jori suddenly remembered hearing stories about starving dogs that had gone wild in the streets, preying on anything weaker than they. For a long minute, neither of them moved.

Don't let it see you're afraid, thought Jori. Yeah. Right.

But the dog didn't do anything. It just sat back on its haunches, closed its mouth, and continued to look at her, its bat-like ears cocked forward, head tilted slightly. Its tail thumped once, as though it were waiting for introductions.

Jori suddenly realized she could no longer hear the footsteps. Or the growls. All right, then. So maybe there was no alley monster, and maybe the dog wasn't looking for dinner. Still, she wasn't safe—not in this place. She started to edge past the animal, which now seemed to be grinning at her.

"Good boy," she said shakily. "Good dog."

She took a deep breath and slid around him, but he jumped to his feet and started trotting by her side. At first, she worried that he might still decide to find out how she tasted. But eventually she relaxed, not entirely unhappy to be in the company of a large dog who could probably make even an ax murderer reconsider his plans.

They reached a slightly wider street, and Jori tried to turn onto it. The dog stopped her, nipping gently at her heels and then shoving his massive shoulder against her hip.

"Listen, dog. I'm not a sheep. And I've got to get home."
He ignored her. Eventually she gave up, thinking that perhaps the dog knew better than she how to find a way back to the main avenue. He nudged her once more, herding her around the next corner.

And that's when she saw it.

A strange light glimmered at the end of the street, blossoming from a stand of ancient oaks that stood like silent giants behind a rough stone wall. The glow warmed the night sky, edging nearby buildings in silver and making the tree trunks gleam as though lit from within.

The dog seemed satisfied. He licked Jori's hand, flashed his sharp-toothed grin, and loped into the shadows at the base of the wall. Jori could barely see him, but she heard him bark once. A voice responded, low and impatient, and the dog disappeared entirely.

Jori squinted, then drooped in relief. Where the dog had vanished, she could just make out a door. And where there was a door, a voice, and a disappearing dog, there had to be people. She ran forward, grabbed the latch, and pulled with all her strength.

The door didn't budge.

"Oh, come on. *Please.*" She noticed a peephole in the center panel and tried to peer through it, but the glass was scratched and cloudy. She pounded furiously on the thick wood, yelling for someone to help her.

Still no response.

"Come on," she whispered again, collapsing against the wooden barrier. "I'm lost, and I'm scared, and I could use a little help."

She heard a whirring sound, felt something writhe against her cheek. She jerked back from the door, slapping at whatever might have crawled out of the wood. Then she froze. The peephole was moving, its glass orb slowly rotating. It stopped, and Jori found herself staring into a single glistening eye.

The eye looked her up and down.

"Excuse me," said a dry, irritated voice, "but I might be more willing to provide some assistance if you didn't pound on me like the proverbial barbarian at the gates."

Jori's jaw dropped. A knothole beneath the eye was moving. Forming words. She squeezed her own eyes shut, hoping she'd reopen them to see only a plain wooden door.

But the voice spoke again. "Well, are you going to say something, or are you under the impression that I'm telepathic?" When Jori didn't answer, the door sighed. "I swear, the dog was more articulate."

Well, at least this explains everything, thought Jori. I've finally gone nuts. She backed away, mind spinning.

"Oh, come now, don't be like that," sighed the door, its gaze softening. "I apologize for my behavior—I suspect I have a touch of dry rot. I'll be happy to let you in. Assuming, of course, that you *do* know how to ask politely."

Jori shook her head, turned, and ran.

TWO
BETRAYAL

Jori wasn't sure how she got home, but for the first time in months she was glad to reach the front door of her house. Just inside, her mom's jacket lay crumpled on the floor next to the banister. Jori heard the *thunk* of a knife on a cutting board and followed the sound into the kitchen. There she found her mom trying to piece together a dinner from leftover chicken, one can of mushroom soup, and a half bag of noodles.

Her mom glanced up when Jori came in, forcing a smile onto her drawn face. Jori hated that smile. It was about as real as a mannequin's.

"Hi, honey. How was school today?"

Jori shrugged, collapsing into a chair and twisting a button on her jacket. "It was okay."

She felt her mom's radar kick in, and a moment later Jori was being examined as meticulously as if she were a crime scene.

"You sure? You look a little—"

"I'm sure."

"Uh-huh." Her mom put down the knife, folded her arms. "Then how about explaining how your hands got torn up? You haven't been fighting with Marisa again, have you?" Jori shook her head, shoving her hands between her knees. "She isn't worth a suspension, honey. Though I swear, when I think of all the dinners I made for that girl . . ."

"It wasn't Marisa. I fell against a wall, that's all." She paused. "Don't worry so much."

"I'm not worried. But since when do you come home and sit in the kitchen with me? Unless cable's off, that is."

Jori shrugged again. Her mom waited a moment longer, then gave up and turned back to the cutting board. "Did you at least pick up the groceries like I asked? I stuck a twenty in your backpack."

Jori cringed. The backpack! Not only did it contain the money, it had her math and lit books, too. Not to mention the forty-some index cards she had compiled for a report that was due in ten days. Now it was all getting soaked in an alley because she'd been spooked by some stupid dog.

"Sorry. I forgot."

"You forgot. You know, Jori, it's hard enough . . ." She stopped. "All right, just give me back the twenty."

"No!"

"Ex*cuse* me?"

"I mean . . . let me hang on to it. I'll pick everything up tomorrow."

Jori waited for another challenge, but her mom simply sighed. "Whatever you say, Jo. But I better not find out you've spent it on something stupid. Or dangerous."

"Like what? Cigarettes? Drugs? I'm not an idiot, Mom."

"No, not drugs." Her mom paused, then walked over to Jori and touched her cheek. "I'm talking . . . chocolate. I've always been worried about your addiction to chocolate." Then she smiled—not the mannequin's smile, either.

Reluctantly, Jori smiled back, wondering if her mother knew how desperately she loved her. If her dad had been the family's bright candy coating, then her mom had always been its sweet center—applauding Jori's successes, listening to Lisa's nonstop chatter, laughing hysterically at every bad joke Jori's dad brought home from work. But all that stopped the day he fumbled for a dropped cell phone while driving Jori to a friend's house. The day their world fell apart.

Jori remembered the endless stream of horror that followed the accident. Waking up in the hospital, wrapped in bandages and in more pain than even the morphine drip could mask. Her mom's haunted face, telling her that her dad was dead and that the funeral had taken place days before. Her first glance in the mirror, when she saw the stitched wounds criss-crossing the right side of her face—wounds she was told could take years of surgeries to erase. She had stared at her reflection for a long time.

Weeks later, when Jori finally returned from the hospital, Lisa met her at the door and grabbed her suitcase, careful not to stare at the angry red scars on her sister's face and arm. They headed toward the bedroom they'd shared almost from the day Lisa was born.

"I turned everything on," Lisa said shyly. "Kind of a welcome back."

But when Jori walked into the room, she stopped dead.

This had always been their sanctuary, a hideaway bursting with the colorful spillover of two very active imaginations. Lisa's side was populated with every imaginary creature she could find—gargoyles and griffins, hobbits and elves, magnificent winged horses and herds of delicate unicorns. After school each day, she would throw her books on the bed and rearrange the miniature figures in endless combinations. When Jori once asked why, she'd grinned. "So they don't get bored."

Jori's contributions were more realistic, but only slightly less extreme. Waterfalls spilled down a whirling lampshade on her desk, while over her bed a dark forest glowed under a light-bulb moon. A sound machine added the music of crickets and the deep chirrups of frogs. And roaming her shelves or staring down from posters on the wall were the wolves. Dozens of them. Ceramic, stuffed, glass, and carved. She had always loved the powerful animals—for their strength, their intelligence, their complete devotion to family.

Until now.

As she stood, staring, the shrill chirps of the frogs and crickets pierced her like short screams. And the wolves, open mouthed and howling, seemed to be laughing at her. Or maybe shrieking. Furious, she began tearing the posters off the wall, yanking the plugs from the chittering sound machines, sweeping the wolves off their shelves to shatter on the floor.

Then, panting, she spun toward Lisa's side of the room, toward her sister's stupid, *stupid*, toys. She knocked over a glittering glass mountain, ripped down the winged unicorn suspended over Lisa's bed, began reaching toward a tiny family of gnomes. She heard a sob, turned, and froze at the agony on Lisa's face.

"Don't," Lisa whispered. "Dad gave me those. Just like he gave you the wolves."

"And Dad's dead," Jori said flatly. "Besides, I have other things to remember him by." She jerked her torn arm up next to her face, watching in grim satisfaction as the last bits of brightness left Lisa's eyes.

From that moment, she went into the room only to sleep. And Lisa seldom left it, sitting on her bed for hours at a time. Jori would sometimes walk by and see her clutching the broken frame of the winged unicorn, her dark eyes like windows to the pain inside.

Summer came, observed by Jori primarily through slits in the mini-blinds. Lisa, too, remained inside, wandering silently from room to room or sitting, unblinking, in front of the TV. And then September forced itself on them, dragging both girls out of the house and back to school. There, Jori found herself firmly in the role of outcast, with people either cringing away from her or ridiculing the way she looked. She sat at the back of classes and walked alone through the halls, where she sometimes spotted Lisa slipping like a wraith through chittering cliques of students. And then, a few weeks later, Lisa didn't come home from school.

Jori remembered her own growing panic that afternoon. Lisa had been coming home later and later each day, but nothing like this. By 5:30, when Lisa still hadn't returned, Jori began calling all of her sister's old friends, even though the last ones had drifted away months before. Then she retraced Lisa's route home, knocking on doors, questioning strangers. No one had seen her. Jori stumbled to the subway station and waited like a statue for her mother to get off the train.

Three hours later they were at the kitchen table, completing a missing person report with the detective who had responded to their call. "Thirteen years old," Jori heard her mother tell the woman. "Long brown hair." Jori couldn't listen. She wandered into the bedroom and sat on Lisa's bed, staring at the empty shelves, the shredded remnants of posters and masking tape on the wall.

Burning at the memory of how she'd abused her sister, Jori reached next to her, groping for the broken unicorn. She felt nothing. Perplexed, she looked down and saw only a slight indentation on the pillow where it usually sat. She stared for a moment, then inspected the rest of the room. Other things were missing, as well. A homemade frame that held a family picture. A treasured children's book. A glass globe in which liquid rainbow colors swirled like clouds. All presents to Lisa from their father.

Jori ran into the kitchen, choking out what she'd discovered. The detective sighed and leaned toward Jori's mom, reaching for her hand. "I know this will be hard for you to hear," she said gently. "But I think we have to consider the possibility that your daughter's run away."

Jori's mom jerked her hand back. "My Lisa wouldn't do that," she said, her eyes straying to a snapshot taped to the refrigerator. In it, a giggling Lisa stood wrapped in the arms of a tall, red-haired man who was making a monster face. "My husband . . . well, he died in a car wreck a few months ago. Ever since then, Lisa's been very quiet. Fragile, even. Where would she get the strength to leave?"

Jori caught the officer glancing at her face. The woman turned quickly away.

"Still . . . sometimes a tragedy like that—"

"My daughter wouldn't run away."

"No," said the officer softly, closing her notebook, "I'm sure she wouldn't."

★ ★ ★

"Go away," Jori whispered to the memory. "You're making me crazy." She got up and set the table, then sat with her mom and forced down a few bites of the makeshift casserole. Later, they huddled in front of the TV, trying to mask the silence of a home that had once rippled with Lisa's laughter and provided a stage for her father's ridiculous, groan-worthy stories.

At least there were no more questions about her backpack or the money. Still, if she wanted to avoid another interrogation, Jori knew she'd better not "forget the groceries" two days in a row.

So the next afternoon, back in detention, she found herself waiting impatiently for Newt. When he finally strolled through the doorway, she waved him over. He walked past her and sat three rows away.

"*Mis*ter McAllister," came the pinched voice of Mr. Alvarez. "I do not believe that's your assigned seat."

"Well, I was hoping you wouldn't mind if I switched. The scenery's better over here."

"Oh, but I do mind, Mr. McAllister. You gave up your right to choose anything when you let those rats out of their cages. Please take your original seat." Mr. Alvarez crossed his arms and waited.

"Jerk," muttered Newt, but he changed desks, pointedly avoiding Jori's eyes.

She let two minutes hum past.

"Hey. Newt."

He ignored her.

"Ps-s-st. Newt. I need to ask you something."

Newt slid down in his seat, and stared at the ceiling.

"Newt. Listen. I'm sorry about yesterday. I acted like a real jerk."

For a moment, he didn't respond. Then he glanced toward her.

"Yeah. You did."

Jori forced a shamed expression onto her face. "I know. Listen, can I talk to you when we get sprung from here? I mean, if I promise not to act like me?"

Newt smiled, finally, then straightened again in his seat. "You bet," he said. "Something up?"

She hesitated. "I need a little favor."

THREE

A DOG WITH A BACKPACK

The ninety minutes crawled by. When the bell finally rang, Newt leaned forward on his desk.

"So, what'd you want to talk about?"

"Let's get outside first."

They walked into the hallway just as Marisa and her entourage came laughing around the corner on their way from the gym. "Shit," Jori muttered, the detention room suddenly seeming attractive. Looking at Marisa's dark eyes, slender 5'7" frame, and flawless olive skin, she immediately felt her scars begin to itch.

"Oh, look," said Marisa, staring at them. "Isn't this just *too* adorable. Jori finally has a boyfriend." Her attendant clones giggled. "And Newt, here everyone thought you weren't interested in girls."

Jori gritted her teeth. "Shut up, Marisa."

"Now, now," said Marisa sweetly, slipping an arm around Jori's waist. "Friends mustn't keep secrets from each other." She leaned closer. "This is big news. One more gay—I mean, guy—on the open market."

"You know, Marisa," Jori said, just as sweetly. "That bruise around your eye is almost gone. How about I freshen it up?"

The other girls shrieked in delighted horror, and Marisa took a quick step backwards. Just then Derek Worsley, Marisa's annointed boyfriend, sauntered around the corner, hands deep in the pockets of his chocolate brown leather jacket. The squeals stopped immediately.

The guy was good looking, even Jori had to admit. He had striking green eyes, perfectly cut hair, and a lean, muscular build. Hard to believe that, less than a year ago, Derek had been a nobody—a dull, sullen boy, slouched at the back of every class, wearing clothes that a homeless shelter would reject.

Then Marisa had spotted him. In need of a slave, she'd evaluated him and decided he could be molded to suit her particular needs. So she flirted with him, stroked his ego, and took him shopping (the leather jacket was her gift to him). Within a month he'd been transformed. Now he'd jump in front of a train if she asked him to.

"Hey, Mar," he said, walking over to them. "Look what I got for you." He pulled a bracelet from his pocket, a gold band with a thin line of crystal chips on both edges. His expression remained guarded until Marisa snatched the bracelet from his fingers, slipped it onto her wrist, and stretched out her arm so her minions could admire it.

"Looks good," said Derek.

"Sure does," Jori agreed. "Whose locker did you lift it from?"

Derek's eyes slid over to her, and he frowned.

"She givin' you trouble, Mar?"

"No. She's just a little testy today. And I'm really not sure why." Marisa smiled. "In fact, I was just telling her what a cute couple she and Newt make. Sort of a scare-crow/munchkin combination."

Derek snorted, and Jori headed toward them, fists clenched. Newt jumped in front of her.

"Excuse me!" he said, staring at Marisa. "Did you just compare me to a skinny, clueless, tap-dancing straw man?" He bowed, sweeping his hand in a huge arc. "I'm flattered." He grabbed Marisa's arms, and began to spin her around, stumbling and slipping through a rubber-limbed waltz as he sang about his lack of a brain.

Marisa shook him off. "God. No wonder everyone thinks you're queer."

Her toadies screamed with laughter, and Newt froze.

Jori stormed over, glaring up into the girl's smug face. "Watch it, Marisa. Believe it or not, you've never seen me get *really* mad."

Marisa looked at Derek expectantly, waiting for him to come to her defense. He stared back blankly, and a flicker of irritation crossed Marisa's face. "You're useless, sometimes, you know that?" Derek's face burned red.

Now Marisa turned again to Jori, her smile back in place. "Well, sweetie, I suppose it's silly for us to fight. In fact," she said, glancing at Newt, "I hope you have a lovely time with this charmer. I understand geeks can be surprisingly competent." She glided off, trailed by her gaggle of admirers.

"Anorexic witch," Jori muttered. "And I think her friends share one brain cell between them." Silently, she and Newt headed from the school. They walked for a block or so, and Jori noticed that Newt looked uncomfortable, seemed to be avoiding her eyes.

"You were terrific," he said finally.

"What?"

"The way you stood up to Marisa. You were great."

Jori shrugged. "No. Just mad. I've got a rotten temper. Which you . . . kind of know already."

A smile twitched across Newt's lips. "Yeah, well, I wish I was more like that. In my head, I can handle myself just great. Punch someone out. Or break a nose, if I have to.

Overcome the evil hordes. But out here, looks like the best I can do is become a dancing scarecrow." He grimaced.

"Listen, Newt. Punching people out is highly overrated. Believe me. Besides, that dance of yours probably saved me from another detention."

"Oh, yeah. I'm a real hero." He switched the subject. "So what is it with you and Marisa, anyhow?" he asked. "How'd that all start?"

None of your business, Jori thought. But she controlled herself, knowing she still needed his help.

"It started back when she first transferred to the school, maybe six months or so before . . . before the accident." Newt's eyes flicked to her face, and she looked away. "I sat next to her in oral communications. She seemed kind of shy then, really insecure. I felt bad for her, so I started talking to her before class every day. One day she just blurted out that she didn't know anyone, that she wished she had a friend like me who could show her around.

"I felt flattered, I guess. Believe it or not, I was pretty popular then. I had lots of friends, played sports, got nominated for a bunch of different clubs and awards. You probably didn't know that."

"Sure I did," said Newt. "I always knew who you were."

Jori paused, surprised. But Newt didn't say anything else. "Anyhow, pretty soon we were together all the time. I introduced her to all my friends, got her involved in the same activities. She was a lot of fun, really, and I kept telling her how great she was, tried to make her feel better about herself."

"Congratulations. You succeeded."

"Yeah, I did. Eventually, she got pretty popular herself. But then she started acting strange. She stopped hanging around with me so much, then not at all. Next thing I knew, she was competing for things I was interested in, and there were all these crazy rumors flying around about me. I couldn't figure it out."

Newt frowned. "Maybe she was afraid."

"Afraid? Of what?"

"Of you. You were the one who'd built her up. Maybe she thought that if she got too popular, you'd tear her back down again."

"Oh, please. I was her best friend, for godssake!" But even as she spoke, Jori realized that something about Newt's comment felt right, like a missing piece snapped into a jigsaw puzzle.

"So?" asked Newt. "Then what happened?"

"Then . . . the accident. While I was in the hospital, she took over everything—my spot on the soccer team, my place on the student board, most of my friends. She never even visited me. And when I finally came back to school, it was like she'd never known me. I was just the freak of the week, someone to make fun of."

"What a pal."

"Yeah."

"So," Newt said, hunching his shoulders and adopting a New Jersey accent, "you wan' I should make her . . . disappear?"

"That'd be nice."

"Okay, den," he said. "Don' you worry 'bout it. Pretty soon she'll be sleeping wit' da fishes."

Jori laughed—then stopped abruptly. They had just reached the intersection of Bridgeview and Fourteenth Street. But the barriers and blinking lights were gone, and there was no sign of construction.

She stared, confused.

"Something wrong?" asked Newt. Jori looked around a few moments longer, then finally told him what had happened the day before. Not the whole story, of course. Just enough to get him to help her retrieve her backpack.

"You sure this is where you were?" Newt asked when she was done

"Yeah, this is it. Bridgeview. At least, I think this is it." She frowned, not sure what to do. She'd figured that they'd start from the barriers, then walk up and down the nearest side streets until she found the one with the broken lamps. But now . . .

A deep bark boomed down the street. Jori stared in astonishment. It was the dog again. And he had one massive paw planted firmly on her backpack.

"Whoa," said Newt. "That's one nasty looking mutt."

"You think so? Well, then we've got a problem." She pointed to the backpack.

"You're kidding."

"Nope, that's it." She moved slowly toward the animal. "Hey, big dog. Whatcha got there?"

The dog's tail wagged slowly. But then he dipped his head, grabbed the straps between his teeth, and began to tug the backpack into the alley. His odd blue eyes dared her to come after him.

"Stop," she said. "Just stop right there!"

The dog ignored her. Turning away, he flipped the heavy bag across his back as easily as if it had been empty. Then he trotted off down the alley, like a student determined not to be late for his next class.

"Get back here!" she yelled, stamping her foot. She looked at Newt. "Come on."

The two of them gave chase, turning into the alley where the dog had disappeared. Moonglow already filled the passage, making it easy for them to follow as the dog trotted through the maze of twists and turns.

"Do you know where he's going?" asked Newt, panting.

"I have an idea."

The dog barked from somewhere up ahead, the sounds bouncing from wall to wall. They ran down another long passage and turned the corner. Light shimmered at the end of the street.

Newt stopped in astonishment. "What *is* that?"

Jori decided she'd let Newt find out for himself. She led him toward the wall, and when they reached the heavy wooden door, she knocked. Hard.

Sure enough, the low whirring sound began, and the glass orb spun into position. The eye appeared, looking perturbed. It glanced first at Newt, then at Jori. Seeing her, it creaked wider.

"You've come back!" The voice from the knothole was bright with pleasure. "I was afraid my rudeness yesterday offended you beyond my power to make amends."

Newt looked shaken. "What's going on?"

"I don't have a clue."

He moved closer, examining the peephole and feeling around the edges of the door. "Okay, so this is one of those electro-anima—those electronic gizmos, right? Like at a theme park. Or there's a hidden camera somewhere, and someone hiding behind a panel."

The door's eye rolled. "Skeptic," it murmured. It turned its attention back to Jori, the brass socket now crinkling pleasantly. "So do tell me, my dear—what brings you back?"

"Uh . . . the dog, basically. He's got my backpack."

The door chuckled softly. "The beast is incorrigible. But if he has your backpack, then I suppose I'll have to let you go in after him, won't I?" She heard a soft click and the scrape of sliding metal. Slowly, the door swung back on its hinges.

"Welcome," it said.

FOUR

THE COLLECTOR

★

Jori stepped through the sagging doorway and stopped, awestruck.

They were in a garden, but a garden unlike any she had ever seen. Slender trees swayed in a warm, lilac-scented breeze, and pure white flowers cascaded from lush tangles of hanging vines. Jori recognized trumpet lilies and roses, hyacinth and azaleas, velvety blankets of silver moss and soft sprays of baby's breath. All glowing brilliant white, and all blooming in the middle of fall, when most should have been long dead.

"It's the Moon Garden," she whispered.

"The what?"

"The Moon Garden. A lullaby my dad made up when Lisa and I were little. We used to sing it with him every night." She closed her eyes, trying to block out the memory she saw blossoming around her. But her father's song forced its way from her, unbidden and unwanted.

> *Come out and play in the Moon Garden*
> *The rest of the world is in bed*
> *Now it's just you and me*
> *And the flowers and trees*
> *And the magical thoughts in our heads.*
>
> *Come sing a song in the Moon Garden*
> *The breezes will pipe on the reeds*
> *And if you'll sing the high notes*
> *Then I will sing low*
> *And we'll see where the melody leads.*
>
> *We're in the Moon Garden, the magic Moon Garden*
> *Caressed by the silver-tipped leaves*
> *Where the trees speak in whispers*
> *And birds never sleep*
> *And you see what you want to believe . . .*

She stopped, feeling a pain she hadn't felt in months. Newt was watching her, his expression gentle.

"It's a nice song, Jori."

Embarrassed, she turned away, wiping angrily at her eyes.

"I don't see our furry friend," she said, struggling to speak past the tightness in her throat. "Hey, big dog. You around?"

"Uh . . ." Newt pointed to the back of the garden. "Maybe he went in there."

Nestled between two large, protective oaks was a small house, a cottage so charming it looked plucked from a storybook. Decorative scrolling edged the low, red-shingled roof, and carved wooden shutters adorned each window. A bright blue door with a lion's head knocker glowed invitingly in the moonlight.

A memory itched at the back of Jori's mind. A vague image of a painting—no, not a painting, one of those "READ" posters. It had hung in the school's resource center when she was little, and she used to stop and look at it every time she visited. She had always loved the little house, dreamed of living in one just like it some day.

Funny, Jori thought, as she and Newt approached the blue door down a short cobblestone path. The artist must have used this house as the model. But she had never imagined anything like this really existed—at least, not in the middle of the city.

Newt reached for the knocker, but the metal hoop floated upward and lightly tapped itself on the wood. Silently, the door swung open.

"Well," said Newt, slowly lowering his hand. "At least this one didn't talk."

Curiouser and curiouser, thought Jori. She peered inside. "Hello? Anyone home?"

There was no response. But Jori, determined to retrieve her backpack, stepped through the doorway.

The room was larger than she would have guessed, and fragrant with the scents of cinnamon and pine. Its walls were a deep moss green, and a beamed ceiling stretched overhead, disappearing into shadows. Four comfortable chairs formed a half-circle around a stone fireplace, while bookcases and curio cabinets claimed the remaining floor space. Colored lights glowed in the darkness from a dozen stained-glass lamps.

Jori glanced into the cabinet beside her. A stuffed squirrel stared back at her with black beady eyes. It was standing alongside an old snow globe, a glass kaleidoscope, the engine from a model train set, and a seashell frame with a picture of a dog in it. Weird, she thought. Why put junk like this in a display case?

She looked at Newt, who was tilting his head and peering at a collection of hardcover novels on one of the shelves.

"Someone's a major fantasy freak. Listen to these titles: *Starship Troopers. The Secret Valley. Jurassic Park. Legends of Old England. Tarzan. The Hobbit . . .*"

An amused voice came from the shadows. "Each a classic, I assure you."

Jori jumped. Smiling at them from a green leather chair was an elderly man. He wore a rumpled, button-down cardigan, tweedy gray pants, and sandals with dark socks. Wisps of long silver hair were combed back neatly on his head, escaping in soft tendrils just above his collar. Gentle eyes peered at them from under salt-and-pepper eyebrows.

A retired teacher, Jori thought immediately. Or Mister Rogers, back from the dead.

"Look, mister," she said, edging back toward the door, "don't call the police. The door was already open, so—"

The old man seemed surprised. "My dear girl. What are you talking about? I'm delighted you're here. In fact, I became quite concerned when you were late. The neighborhood has suffered regrettable changes over the years, and one never knows what one will encounter in the streets."

Jori stopped. "What do you mean, late? We didn't know we were coming here."

"I'm not surprised. Few people do."

"Then what—"

"Why don't I begin by showing you around?" said the old man, slowly pushing his frail frame from the chair and reaching for a wooden cane.

Jori started again. "But wait, we don't know anything about—"

"Nor would I expect you to. Hence, my plan to serve as your instructor." He patted her arm encouragingly. "Don't be embarrassed, my dear. I can see you're quite intelligent, and I'm sure you'll learn quickly. Now, then. Shall we begin? I'm sure you're most eager to see my collections."

He's nuts, Jori thought, looking at Newt out of the corner of her eye. He circled a finger by his ear, then gestured to her to be careful.

Jori forced a smile. "Collections," she said. "Sure. That sounds great."

"I imagine it does. Now, then, let me see." He looked around, thrumming his fingers against his lips. Then he smiled. "Ah, yes. The perfect thing for your friend. Young man. Please follow me."

Newt raised an eyebrow, but walked toward the old man. Jori trailed just behind. On the wall opposite them was a spectacular display of ancient battle equipment—massive broadswords and breastplates, vicious-looking pikes, helmets and shields, maces and morningstars. Newt's jaw dropped.

"This is . . . wow." He looked at the old man curiously. "How'd you know I was into this kind of thing? It's not exactly common knowledge."

His host smiled. "Good instincts." He then began a detailed explanation of the various items, explaining their history, purposes, and construction to his fascinated guest. As he lectured, Jori wandered to a set of flat glass display cases. She peered inside, then bent closer in surprise.

Expertly arranged on beds of soft cotton was an extraordinary insect collection. Jori could see every type of bug imaginable, from delicate dragonflies and tiny aphids to fierce-looking rhinoceros beetles. She was especially fascinated by a spectacular display of moths and butterflies. As she studied them, the old man walked up next to her.

"These are really something," she said, her apprehension temporarily forgotten.

"My lepidoptera? Yes, they are lovely, aren't they."

Jori scanned the other cases. "No spiders, though. I know it's strange, but I like spiders."

"I don't think that's strange at all," he said. "I admire them as well. But spiders are not insects, you see. They are actually arachnids, a type of arthropod. So I could never put one in a case with a common cicada, now could I?"

"I suppose not."

"Besides, somehow it doesn't seem right to trap spiders behind glass. They should be left alone, free to spin their magnificent webs. Don't you think so?" He touched her shoulder.

Jori jerked away, her nervousness back full force. But the old man was looking at her with nothing other than kindness.

She remembered her initial distrust of Newt. Maybe it's me, she thought. Maybe everyone's perfectly fine and I'm paranoid. To make amends, she affected interest in the rest of the old man's treasures. "You've got a little of everything here. Dolls, old books, music boxes . . . Is this a museum or something?"

"Or something," he nodded, apparently unoffended by her brief reaction. "I am an avid collector."

"But where did you get it all?"

"An excellent question, my dear, but difficult to answer. You see, I've been collecting for a long time." His eyes seemed to lose their focus. "A very long time."

Newt walked up beside them. "You have any other collections like that, Mister—?"

"Professor, actually. Professor DePris."

I was right, thought Jori. "Professor of what?"

"Of humanity, I suppose you'd say. I study people—their lives, their struggles, their desires. It's endlessly fascinating—my food and drink, in some ways." He smiled at Jori, then turned back to Newt. "Now then, you were asking about the weapons. Yes, I have many more that would interest you, I'm sure. But first, why don't we relax a moment? I've prepared a lovely repast."

He gestured graciously toward a low wooden table that stood by the fireplace. It had a broad, highly polished surface and four thick legs that ended in carved lion's paws. It also had nothing on it.

Jori looked at the empty table, her anxiety returning. "Thanks for the offer, Professor. But we really just came to get my backpack."

"Are you sure, my dear?"

"I'm sure. We've got to go." She felt a twinge of guilt at his look of disappointment. "Besides, there's . . . nothing *on* the table."

"Of course there—" He stopped, staring at the gleaming wooden surface. "Blast. You're right. Although I don't know why I'm surprised. Good serving tables are so hard to find these days." He gave an exasperated sigh, then walked over to the table and tapped it sharply with his cane. "Must I always remind you?"

Jori whispered in Newt's ear. "Okay, we're out of here. This guy's either nuts or—"

She stopped, eyes riveted to the table. Three domed silver platters were now neatly arranged on its gleaming surface, along with three sets of silverware in crisp linen pockets.

"Yes, my dear?" said the old man solicitously. "Did you say something?"

Jori just shook her head. This was getting way too weird. Newt, too, was silent.

"In that case," said the old man, "why don't we sit by this beautiful fire and chat a bit while you enjoy your refreshments?"

Jori looked weakly at the empty fireplace. "Fire?"

There was a soft *poof!* and a tiny forest of flames leaped upwards in the grate. Jori jumped. But she saw a small smile slip onto Newt's face.

The Professor ushered them politely toward the chairs. Newt quickly chose one and sank with a sigh into the plush velvet cushions. Jori hesitated, still nervous. But the chair didn't move, talk, or appear to do anything else unusual, so she warily sat down in the seat next to Newt's. The pillows squirmed to match her shape, and she yelped. Newt laughed.

The old man remained standing. He seemed to be waiting for something, and Jori's nerves went back on orange alert.

"Aren't you going to join us?" Newt asked.

"Of course. But it's only polite to wait until your friend arrives."

"What friend?"

"The one looking in the window."

Jori and Newt whipped around, just in time to see a sculpted hairline dip below the sill.

"Derek," they said in unison.

"Marisa must have told him to follow us," fumed Jori. "To bring back a little manure to spread around school tomorrow."

"Oh, no," said the professor. "I don't think so. I suspect he's just waiting to be invited in." He turned his head. "Gopher! May I see you for a moment?"

Jori heard paws scrabbling across polished wood, and the big dog from the alley skidded into the room. He bounded over to Jori, panted happily in her face, then galumphed back to the old man, sliding to a stop at his feet. His tongue slipped from his mouth in excitement.

"Gopher," Newt said, and the dog's tail thumped. "Strange name for a dog, isn't it?"

"Not at all. You see, he'll *go-fer* anything I ask him to." The old man chuckled, then turned back to the dog. "Gopher, there's a young man just outside the window. Would you please invite him to join us?"

Gopher's tongue snapped back into his mouth like a window-shade, and he leaped for the door. It opened just as he approached it. There was a startled yell, a low growl, and a few moments later Gopher's rear end reappeared, jerking as his other end tugged at something.

"All *right!*" a voice snarled. "Don't ruin the leather! I'm coming, you friggin' mutt."

A moment later, Gopher backed into the room, his nose wrinkled in disgust. He was followed by a scowling Derek. When they were both inside, the dog sniffed at him, gagged slightly, then looked over at the old man.

"Thank you, Gopher. That was splendid."

Gopher wagged his tail. Then he trotted over to Jori, plopped down next to her, and laid his big head in her lap. Finally succumbing to his charm, Jori slipped him a crumbled cookie from her pocket. He gulped it down and looked at her worshipfully.

Derek glared at the Professor.

"Mister, I could sue you. That dog tried to kill me."

"Oh, I doubt that, my boy."

"Yeah? Well, look at these bite marks." Derek pulled fiercely at the sleeves of his jacket. "Marisa's gonna go apeshit."

"Don't worry," said Jori. "You can always steal another one."

"Yeah? Well you can—"

"Now, now," said Prof. DePris, "No harm has been done, and our refreshments are waiting. Mr. Worsley, won't you please join Jori and Nathaniel at the table?"

Derek looked confused. "Join who?"

"Wait a minute," Jori said. She looked at Newt, who was staring at the old man. "Your name is Nathaniel?"

"What?" He glanced at her distractedly. "Oh . . . yeah. Nate, for short. But the only one who ever used it was my mom." His eyes returned to the old man. "Who . . . How did you know?"

"Why, I wouldn't be a very good host if I didn't know your name, now would I? That's one of the most elementary rules of etiquette."

"Nathaniel," repeated Derek slowly, apparently trying to file the name away in his mind. "That's great."

Jori's shot him a murderous look. "You say anything—" She reconsidered. "What am I worried about? Your brain can't handle words longer than two syllables."

"Bite me," replied Derek.

The old man raised one hand.

"Please, Mr. Worsley, do sit back down. I assure you, Nathaniel and Jori are both smart, congenial young people."

"There's no way I'm joining some friggin' tea party."

"Derek," Jori said, the strain of dealing with both him and the old man sawing across her nerves. "Just shut up and *sit down!*"

Derek's jaw dropped. But he slumped into a chair, leaving one seat between himself and Jori.

The old man beamed at the three of them. "Well, isn't this lovely," he said. He gestured toward the three covered platters. "Now please, my friends—enjoy."

Jori hesitated. But Newt, the odd expression once again on his face, lifted the silver dome in front of him. For some reason, Jori couldn't quite identify what had been revealed. But Newt smiled broadly, an unvoiced expectation met.

"Barbecued turkey leg and roasted corn on the cob," he said. "Pretty much my all-time favorites." He grinned at the old man, then took a huge, sloppy bite of the turkey leg that Jori suddenly had no trouble seeing.

Curious now, she uncovered her own platter. In front of her, hot fudge dripping down its sides, was a triple fudge brownie topped with chocolate ice cream, chocolate chips, and crumbled Oreo cookies.

"Chocolate Decadence," she murmured.

The old man nodded. "Another favorite, I believe?"

Derek now seemed to forget about displaying attitude. He lifted the silver cover and peered under it.

"Sardines and peanut butter on crackers."

Whoa, thought Jori. There's been a glitch in the Matrix.

But Derek seemed pleased. "I haven't had this since I was a kid," he said, to himself more than to any of them. He snatched up a cracker, set it on his tongue, and chewed slowly.

The old man turned back to Jori, who hadn't yet touched her food. "Why, what's wrong, my dear? Aren't you hungry?"

Of course she was. But she wasn't stupid, either. How had the old man managed to have their favorite foods ready when none of them had even known they were coming? How could she be sure that the chocolate wasn't laced with drugs, or masking some kind of poison? On the other hand, she thought, Derek and Newt weren't in convulsions on the floor yet . . .

"Sure I'm hungry," Jori replied, deciding to humor the old man a little longer. "I was just a little surprised." She carved off a small chunk of the brownie and took a taste. As soon as it touched her tongue, her body began to melt with pleasure. It was the richest, creamiest, most astonishing chocolate she had ever tasted.

She was soon the only one eating. Newt sat sprawled in his chair, his eyes drooping, a satisfied smile on his face. Derek's head was flopped back against the cushion, a half-eaten cracker still in one hand. Seeing them, Jori stopped in mid-chew.

She stole a glance at Mr. DePris, who was rummaging through a cubby in an old roll-top desk. She scooped the remaining dessert into her napkin and folded it in half. One big chunk of brownie escaped and fell to the floor, but Gopher immediately gobbled it down. Jori sank back into the cushions, letting her eyes droop slightly.

She watched the old man return to the fire, a small velvet pouch clasped in one hand. He gazed silently at his guests, then settled into the one empty chair, humming softly.

"Isn't it lovely," he said, "to gather around a cheerful fire for a satisfying meal and pleasant conversation?" Jori saw Newt nod sleepily.

"But," the old man continued, "what I really treasure, even more than conversation, is a good story. And in all modesty, I must say that I am quite a spinner of tales. Would you be interested in hearing one?" Jori, who was vaguely aware that her eyes had closed, was surprised to feel herself nod.

"Wonderful. Let me take just a moment to set the mood." Jori forced her eyes open again in time to see the old man's right hand move in a smooth half circle, the fingers closing gracefully over his palm. The stained glass lamps dimmed, leaving the room in a pleasant half light.

He slipped his fingers into the velvet pouch and brought out a handful of sparkling crystals. These he tossed into the fire. Soon, the flames flashed with sparks of blood-red ruby, dark sea sapphire, and rich emerald green. A warm wave of comfort flowed over Jori's skin, and she smelled the sweet green fragrance of spring nights and rain-washed breezes.

"And now," said the old man, leaning back in his chair, "I'll spin you a story. One you know, but haven't heard."

"That's not possible," murmured Jori.

"Are you certain, my dear?" the old man asked, looking at her speculatively. "I myself am never sure of what's possible." He paused, and Jori watched the flames begin to swirl out of the fireplace, encircling them.

"Look into the fire, my young friends." The professor's voice was as soft and soothing as snow falling on water. "Look . . . and dream . . . and you'll begin to see my story."

FIVE

DREAMFIRE

Jori's comfortable chair began to rock and weave, the floor beneath it billowing like waves on a silent sea. Around her, the room grew less substantial, melting into streams of color that swirled and spiraled like tinted oils in a kaleidoscope. A cool breeze danced through her hair, and she looked up to find that the ceiling had vanished, replaced by a tangle of stars in a moon-brushed sky.

She drifted out of her chair and reached toward the stars, which spun above her in an intricate dance. Then a strange song drifted up next to her, slipping itself gently into her mind.

> *Sing your songs and dream your dreams*
> *Seek your heart's desire.*
> *Hear the whispers of your soul*
> *Warm them by the fire.*

Captivated by the melody, Jori looked down and saw her own body curled beneath her in the chair. She could see Newt and Derek as well, wrapped in cocoons of sleep. And then she found the music.

It was the old man, of course, his voice as hypnotic as the Pied Piper's flute.

> *Lay them out for all to see*
> *Deepest secrets share*
> *They will be your gift to me*
> *Given unaware . . .*

"Finish," she whispered, her sleeping self forming the words.

For a moment, there was no reply.

"Did you say something, dear?"

"Given . . . unaware. Unaware . . . of what?"

"Nothing, my dear. It was a song without an ending. I never know the endings."

"But . . ."

"Sleep, my sweet. Sleep, if you want to hear the story."

The stars spiraled off into darkness. Of course she wanted to hear the story. She always did, even though she had just turned eight and was really much too old for fairy tales. She sat cross-legged on her bed, wriggling happily as her father plucked the beloved book from the shelf.

Next to her, Lisa was jumping up and down on the mattress, pigtails bouncing. Jori yanked on the edge of her sleep shirt.

"Watch out, Lisa," she whispered in mock-terror. "Here he comes!" Lisa collapsed next to her, giggling and clutching the new winged unicorn she'd just received for her birthday. A moment later, their dad bellowed like Tarzan, swooped down between them, and launched a dastardly tickle attack. They screamed with laughter, beating on his shoulders, gasping for breath, and pleading for mercy. Suddenly he straightened.

"All right, all right, that's enough. A great actor such as *moi* cannot concentrate with this kind of behavior in the audience. Although perhaps I could be persuaded if someone gave me a scroonch." They flung their arms around him and squeezed, and he kissed the tops of both their heads. Then he picked up the book, put one hand on his chest, and cleared his throat four times.

"*The Secret Valley*," he announced grandly. His voice grew softer. "In the greenest of the green forests of Avendar, there lived a lone wolf . . ."

Jori listened as her father read, loving his deep, rumbly voice even more than she loved the story. The book was their favorite, a treasure that had both wolves and unicorns in it. Closing her eyes, she could imagine every glittering detail.

"It sounds so pretty," said Lisa dreamily. "Daddy, could you take us there someday?"

"Someday? How about now?" He strode across the room to the closet, flung open the door, and swept his arm toward the opening. Sunrise spilled into the room, and the laughter of waterfalls. Lisa grabbed Jori's hand, pulling her through the doorway.

They emerged at the edge of a whispering forest, their feet crunching fallen leaves the color of spun candy. The air was delicious with the scent of peppermint, and a bright stream splashed out of the nearby woods. Suddenly Lisa clapped her hands.

"Jori, look! There it is!"

On the other side of an amber meadow, past a rise of blue-velvet hills, a magnificent crystal mountain reached joyfully into the clouds.

"Come on," gasped Lisa. They raced toward the mountain, arms out like wings so they could brush the feathery tips of the grasses. Jori's heartbeat quickened as they reached the gentle hills, ran up the sides, and stopped spellbound at the top.

The valley lay before them like a gift. Clusters of pink clover covered its sides, and a sea of white crocus and pale lavender billowed across the valley floor. Streams from the Crystal Mountain leaped down the transparent cliffs, bursting into rainbows of mist on the rocks below.

And everywhere, absolutely everywhere, were the unicorns.

They filled the valley, magnificent horse-creatures that seemed molded from living ivory. White manes glimmered like sea spray above their arched necks, and their horns were bright slivers of moonlight. From their chins, soft beards floated, and feathery tufts of hair almost hid their cloven hooves.

Jori and Lisa started down the hill, and the unicorns whinnied bell-like greetings. But something oozed at the edge of Jori's vision and she lifted her head, uneasy. A black cloud was rising behind the mountain, boiling over its sides, blocking out the light. The streams flowing down the once-bright cliffs turned black, and as Jori watched in horror, they seeped into the meadow, poisoning the grasses along the banks and raising the stench of death. Jori reached for her sister's hand.

Lisa was gone.

"No!" moaned Jori. "Not again."

A flash of light startled her, and she saw a large silver wolf standing silently just a few feet away. Its dark eyes captured and held her own, and in a moment she forgot her anguish. Then the valley itself vanished, and Jori once more found herself floating several feet above her own sleeping body. The two boys remained asleep as well. Even Gopher was stretched on his side, snoring.

Something else caught her eye. Faint shapes hovered above each sleeping form, ghostly images shimmering in the dim light. Over Newt's head, two broadswords flashed, and a powerful man stood silhouetted on a hilltop. Above Derek was the slender form of a beautiful young woman. She was wrapped in gold cloth, and wearing some kind of crown.

Comic book Amazon, Jori thought. Or maybe a porn star.

She heard a soft yip and looked at the dog. Even Gopher had his phantoms. Over his head were cookies and a rabbit and . . . Jori squinted. It seemed to be a picture of her.

The old professor sat motionless in his chair, staring at the floating images. "Exquisite," he murmured. "And well worth the wait. Don't you agree, my sweet?"

Jori shivered. Who was he talking to? As she watched, four slender legs stretched themselves from the pocket of his sweater, attached to an almost transparent body. He stroked the legs absently with one finger. "You'll do wonders with these, won't you, my friend?"

His gaze wandered over to Jori. He started, body tensing, as if he knew that she'd seen. The long legs twitched back into his pocket. But then he relaxed and smiled, waving a gentle hand in her direction. The dizziness returned, and she drifted once more in a pleasant, dreamless darkness.

Much later, she woke to the touch of a wet nose—Gopher nuzzling her hand. Newt and Derek were awake, too, but sitting motionless and staring at nothing. The fire still crackled cheerily, and the old man waited patiently in his chair.

"Well," he said finally, his smile somewhat mischievous. "Did you all enjoy the story?"

Newt looked up, his face a question. "Yeah. I did." He paused. "It was . . . about a battle, right?"

"No," whispered Derek, green eyes feverish. "It was—" He stopped, eyes narrowing, and retreated into silence.

Jori bit her lower lip, a knot forming in her stomach. Somehow, they had each heard or seen something different. She tried to hide her growing nervousness, but Mr. DePris caught her eye, looked at her knowingly. Then he winked.

"Well now. I believe Jori suspects that my humble entertainment is a bit more elaborate than I had implied. And truthfully, I do have a confession to make." He leaned forward, resting his chin on steepled fingers. "The stories shared around this fire aren't mine at all."

"What do you mean?" asked Newt.

"Think for a moment. Didn't it all seem quite familiar?"

Like an album of my memories, thought Jori. She saw Newt's gaze turned inward, as though he were watching a movie in his mind.

"It was something I've imagined a hundred times," he said finally. "But how did you . . . ?"

"It's rather hard to explain," said the old man. "But long ago, during my studies, I learned a precious secret. With just the right combination of ingredients—food for the body, songs for the heart, light and warmth for the soul—one can unlock the deepest secrets of what remains. The mind."

Jori suddenly understood. "You mean our dreams."

"Clever girl. Yes, my dear. Your dreams."

Derek's face twisted into its usual sneer.

"Dreams. Right. What a load of—"

"Shut up, Derek," Newt said, startling Jori. "Why don't you try *not* being an asshole for two minutes?" The two boys jumped to their feet and glared at each other, Derek's right hand curled into a fist.

The old man rose, murmuring soothingly. "Now, now. I'm not offended, Nathaniel, so please don't you be. Derek is simply a young man who knows the value of unfettered expression. Isn't that so, Derek?"

"Sure," said Derek, still glowering at Newt. "Whatever."

"In any case, there *is* more to all of this. What I've shown you is only the beginning. Upstairs, you see, is my finest collection, and my greatest treasure. Would you care to see it?"

Derek didn't reply, but his fist relaxed and he turned away from Newt. To Jori's dismay, Newt also responded. And then she saw his eyes. They were bright with excitement—excitement, and an almost desperate hope.

This is *not* good, Jori thought, feeling a little sick. The strange house, the half-answered questions, Newt's odd behavior—all of it too unnerving. And now, was she supposed to just follow the old man up to some room and let him turn them into tomorrow's headlines?

"It's getting pretty late," she said. "My mom will be home soon."

Derek sneered. "Oh. And will Mommy worry?"

"Yeah, she will. Mothers do that. Or don't they have mothers where you and the rest of the pond scum live?"

The old professor broke in. "Now, friends, there's no need to quarrel. Jori, you are quite right, my dear. It *is* getting late, and we shouldn't cause your mother one moment of worry. Not with what she's already been through."

"Wait. How did you—"

"Nor should we rush what I have to show you," he continued smoothly. "You can always come back another time."

The knot in Jori's stomach finally relaxed. But Derek kicked at a chair leg, and Newt wouldn't look at her. His hands were clenched at his sides.

Only Mr. DePris seemed untroubled. "So then. When may I look forward to your company again?"

"How about tomorrow?" Newt said, before Jori could draw a breath.

"Tomorrow? Tomorrow would be perfect. I'll look forward to it." He paused. "Also . . . well, I know this will sound a little odd, but may I ask a favor?"

"Sure," said Newt. "What do you need?"

"Well, you now know what a passionate collector I am. And the things I treasure most are gifts from my friends, bits of their lives that reflect who they are. A holdover from my years of research, I suspect. So tomorrow, when you return, would you each do me the honor of bringing a memento of some kind? Something that says who you are, or perhaps what you dream of being."

What a weird thing to ask, Jori thought. She saw Newt nod, though, and Derek shrugged noncommitally.

"Lovely," said the professor. "Thank you all so much for indulging an old man." Gopher suddenly scrambled up next to him, his tail wagging proudly as he offered Jori something that dangled from his mouth.

"Ah, yes," said Mr. DePris. "You mustn't forget your backpack."

SIX
THE TREASURE UPSTAIRS

★

The cottage door clicked shut behind them, and Derek jerked away, bolting toward the alley. But just before he reached the stone wall, he stopped.

"Listen," he said. "I want to get a look at whatever it is that the old fart has upstairs. So I'll be back tomorrow, too."

Jori folded her arms.

"Fingers feeling a little sticky, Derek?"

He ignored her. "You two just make sure you keep your mouth shut about everything. Whatever the old guy's got . . .

I don't want anyone else finding out about it." He disappeared through the garden door.

"Nice guy," said Newt. "Wonder what rock he lives under."

For a few minutes, the two of them walked in silence. Then Newt glanced at her.

"So. What's the matter? Besides Derek, I mean."

"I'm not sure. Just too much weirdness back there, I guess. The door, the garden. That little snack that came out of nowhere. And whatever it was that happened around the fire."

"Yeah, it was weird. But a lot more interesting than cable and AOL, right?"

"I don't know. Maybe I'm just a little paranoid after the last few months."

Newt stopped in his tracks.

"I'm a jerk, Jori. I forgot about your sister."

"It's okay."

"No, you're right. Look, we don't have to go back tomorrow, if you don't want to."

Jori felt a rush of relief. But when she looked at Newt, his expression didn't match his words. She struggled for a moment, trying to dissect her own discomfort. There was definitely something off about the old man and his house. But was there really anything dangerous? She thought a moment longer, then pictured the too-quiet house she'd be going home to otherwise, and her mother's mannequin smile.

"I guess the old guy was harmless enough. I mean, I don't think we'll end up buried in his basement or anything."

"Great!" Newt caught himself. "I mean . . . at least it's something different."

So the next afternoon, Jori reluctantly found herself walking through the twisted sidestreets for the third time in as many days. Actually, she was almost sprinting, since Newt seemed to be using every inch of his long legs to cover the distance to the old man's house as quickly as possible.

"So, Newt," she said, attempting to slow him down. "Show me what you brought for the old guy's collection."

He smiled, then pulled an old DVD case from his pocket. On the front was a picture of a long-haired warrior standing on a bloody battlefield.

"*Braveheart,*" Newt said. "It's about a guy named William Wallace. Defender of freedom, savior of Scotland."

"I know. My mom rented it once. So, this is your favorite thing?"

"Of course." He leaned close to her, whispering. "See, I try to keep it quiet, but I *am* William Wallace, reincarnated. Allow me to demonstrate."

He picked up a rusted car antenna and crouched low, looking warily around the alley. A moment later he uttered a wild battle cry and lunged toward a nearby garbage can. Reaching the apparently hostile container, he attacked viciously, stabbing and slashing, showing no mercy until it lay on its side, its trashy guts spilled on the wet pavement.

Jori applauded, and Newt bowed. He tossed the antenna back on the ground and looked again at his DVD. "Really, though, I love this stuff. People fighting for a cause, willing to die for what they believe in. And then, of course, Wallace is your basic hero—strong, determined, fearless. In other words, the opposite of me."

He stopped, his face a little red. "Come on," he said. "Don't want the old guy to worry."

When they reached the wooden door that guarded the entrance to the garden, the metal socket creaked open without Jori even having to knock.

"Well, hello again!" the door said, its glass eye sparkling. "Getting to be regulars, aren't you?"

"It's your a-*door*-able personality," said Newt. "How could we stay away?"

"There's hope for you yet, boy," chuckled the door. It winked and swung open into the garden.

Like another bit of magic, Derek materialized beside them.

"Hey," he said awkwardly.

"Hey," replied Newt. Jori didn't bother to reply, just walked forward.

The cottage door was already open. Gopher waited just outside the entrance, his tail wagging and his eyes glued to Jori's pocket.

"Yeah, I'm ready for you," she said, and brought out a half-eaten sandwich that she'd saved from lunch. The dog snarfed it down, stood on his hind legs, and dragged his tongue across her face. Grinning, she shoved him back down.

"Thanks, big dog. But next time, just give me your paw."

Gopher wriggled happily, then ushered them inside to where Mr. DePris sat quietly by the fire. Gopher barked, and the old man turned.

"My dear friends!" His face was bright with pleasure. "And Jori. I'm especially happy to see you, my dear."

For some reason, she shivered when he singled her out.

"Now please, come warm yourselves by the fire. I'll order your refreshments." He leaned over the serving table, tapping once on the dark wood surface. "Would you be so kind—"

"I'm not hungry," said Derek.

The old man looked perplexed.

"Amazing. I thought hunger was a perpetual condition in young men."

"It usually is," said Newt, jumping in as though he and Derek had planned the dialogue. "But we grabbed something on the way over." Jori tilted her head at the lie, then saw Newt's eyes stray over to the nearby staircase, which curved up into the shadows.

Suddenly she understood. The old man did, as well.

"Well of course, of course! You're simply eager to see my treasure." He reached for his cane, then pulled himself up from his chair. "I don't blame you for being impatient— after all these years, it still makes my own heart race. Please, my friends, follow me." Smiling, he lead them toward the staircase and began to climb. Newt was almost on his heels, Jori and Derek trailing just behind.

Suddenly Gopher forced his way past Derek and thrust himself in front of Jori. He shoved his head against her leg, whimpering.

"Sorry, Gopher," she said, bending down and tugging playfully on his ears. "I'm all out of food."

The old man turned, looking down at them. He was no longer smiling. Jori straightened, feeling that either she or the dog must have done something wrong. "Now, Gopher," he said finally, "you know you're not allowed on the second floor."

Gopher whined softly. Then he nuzzled Jori's hand and slunk back down the stairs.

"He's a good dog," said the professor, "but he's been responsible for more than his share of torn linens and broken vases." The smile returned, and once again he began climbing toward the shadows.

Jori heard a startled noise from Newt. Looking up, she saw that the stairs had come to a dead end at the ceiling—but that half of the old man had already disappeared through the wood. All that was visible were his legs, which were still climbing.

Newt laughed softly. "Sure," he said. "Why not?" He continued up the stairs and soon, just like the old man, began to disappear through the wooden planks.

Jori stared, open mouthed. No, no, this was insane. It was like the old man was stripping away reality, one layer at a time. Getting them ready for . . . something.

"Okay. That's it." She tried to retreat, but backed into Derek, whose arms were stretched from banister to banister. He leaned toward her.

"Forget it, Jori. If you leave, then the old guy will come back down to find out what happened. Which'll mean I won't get to check out whatever he's got upstairs. And that'd make me real unhappy." He stared a challenge directly into her eyes.

Jori glared right back. But then she realized that she couldn't just leave Newt up there to . . . whatever. Not when she'd been the one to drag him to the house in the first place. Without another word, she turned, squeezed her eyelids shut, and darted up the next few steps. She felt something press against her head, then melt away and slide down her face and arms.

When she finally opened her eyes, she had pushed through to the second floor. At least, her top half had. She felt an impatient shove on her rear end and kicked beneath her until she hit something. Stepping quickly up onto the floor, she turned in time to watch Derek materialize through the wood, rubbing his head and scowling. But then his green eyes lit with interest.

Newt and the old man waited just a few feet away, next to a door that was stained a deep, rust red and varnished to an almost metallic smoothness. In the center, a mosaic of tiny colored stones formed a strange symbol that Jori had never seen before—two connected circles, one large and one small, with four angled lines stretching out from each side of the smaller one.

"So, this is where you keep it?" asked Derek.

"Yes." The old man looked at his three guests affectionately. "And now, if you would indulge me—I must ask you to close your eyes."

Derek snorted, and Jori's shoulders tensed. But they all did as told. Silence enveloped them, and Jori heard the door whisper open. Once again she felt a comforting warmth flow around her, smelled the fresh, clean scent of rain. A hand brushed her cheek, and she jumped.

"What—"

"Shhh," said the old man, his voice shifting into the same melodic tone he had used around the fire. "Just relax. Breathe deeply. Let your thoughts drift free. For in this room is a treasure beyond imagining. But your heart must be eager, and your mind willing."

Jori relaxed, just slightly, and felt an odd pull from the direction of the open door. She heard two sets of hesitant footsteps as the boys were guided inside the room. Then she felt the old man's hands on her own shoulders, leading her forward.

"Now open your eyes, my dear young friends. Open you eyes—and see my treasure."

At first, Jori found she couldn't obey him. But then she heard Derek's voice, squeezing from between clenched teeth.

"What the *hell*? Are you freakin' *kidding* me?"

Jori opened her eyes.

They were standing in a large room, dimly lit by an ivory orb that floated just below the ceiling. But this room held no comfortable chairs, no oak cabinets, no fascinating collections. All Jori could see were rough wood floors and blank plaster walls. And a thick, carpet-like hanging that covered one wall entirely.

"This sucks," muttered Derek. "I blow off Marisa to come stare at a rug."

Newt looked at him in disgust, though his own disappointment was obvious. "Shut up, Derek. Some rugs are really valuable, like—"

"Rug." The old man's voice sounded flat, icy, and Jori turned to see dark shadows chasing across his face. "Is that all you see?"

She felt a stab of fear. Stupid, stupid—she should have known better than to come back here. Half the psychos in the world probably seemed harmless until you pushed the wrong button.

Rushing toward the wall, she scrambled for something positive to say, some way to calm him before he became violent. "They're morons, Professor. Just ignore them. It's beautiful, really! It's—"

She stopped, staring. And then forgot to breathe.

What hung before her on the wall—a tapestry, she suddenly remembered these things were called—was something very different than what she had expected. Its threads glimmered as though spun from jewels, and woven into its design were a hundred exquisitely detailed scenes. But it was more than artistry or craftsmanship that set this tapestry apart.

The pictures were alive.

Where Jori's eyes were riveted, trees actually swayed in a soft breeze, and tiny winged lizards hopped along their branches. High above the forest canopy, dragons with human riders twisted through a tumble of clouds, ruby flames blazing from their mouths.

She felt Newt and Derek draw next to her, but by now she was too lost in the images to speak to them. In one scene, ships sailed across frenzied seas, their captains searching for the drowned city of Atlantis that gleamed in the dark waters beneath. In another, a band of determined warriors wandered through a deadly maze of tunnels, an image that reminded Jori of a video game she once played. And higher on the fabric, on a purple and green landscape, spotted creatures with three horns galloped under the light of twin moons.

"It's . . . unbelievable," Jori murmured.

"Yes. It is." Mr. DePris stood just a few steps away, his voice gentle once again. "Please accept my apologies for my reaction just now. I suppose I'm far too sensitive when it comes to this particular piece." His eyes wandered to the tapestry. "It is magnificent, though, isn't it? And as changeable as the dreamers who dream it."

The odd phrase bothered Jori. "What do you mean, 'the dreamers who dream it'?"

"I'm surprised, my dear. I thought that you, at least, would have guessed."

She shook her head, her eyes still holding the question.

"My tapestry is not like any other. Those are poor creations of thread and silk, now moldering in trunks or gathering dust in museums. But this one is woven from much more precious materials."

"What?" Jori whispered.

"From dreams."

She started, then looked toward the two boys. Newt seemed almost hypnotized by what he was hearing. But Derek's face was dark with frustration.

"Tell you what," he said. "If I decide to look at hallucinations, I'll buy some mind candy and see my own."

Mr. DePris clicked his tongue. "And put yourself at risk? Besides, why would you be satisfied with just watching your dreams?"

Derek looked as though his head were going to explode. But Newt's face took on an almost desperate expression. "Tell me what you mean."

"Didn't you notice?" The old man gestured toward a faded section of the cloth from which all of the colors seemed to have drained. "The tapestry is not quite complete. It never is."

"Okay. So?"

"So. It is there that we will weave *your* dreams. And then you will go in and live them."

SEVEN

INTO THE TAPESTRY

★

"Live our dreams?" Newt stared at the tapestry, and Jori realized that nothing existed for him now except the shifting images and the old man. "But . . . how?"

"It's quite simple, really. Just a matter of skill, artistry, and imagination. You supply the imagination. My friend and I will supply the rest."

Friend, thought Jori, eyeing the shadows nervously. Who has he got hiding up here?

But Mr. DePris simply pulled at the pocket of his sweater and peered into the opening. "Arachnea, my dear, would you come out, please?"

A long thin leg poked itself out of the pocket. Then another. And another. And five more. All moving in graceful, languid arcs and connected to an almost transparent body. When the spider had emerged completely, it crawled to the old man's right shoulder and settled there. Jori suddenly understood what the symbol on the red door meant.

"This," said the old man respectfully, "is Arachnea. She is perhaps the most brilliant weaver it has ever been my good fortune to know. It is she who is responsible for what you see in my tapestry."

"Wait a minute," said Jori, trying desperately to inject some semblance of reality. "You expect us to believe that a spider wove this whole thing?"

"*Are you questioning my abilities, human?*" Jori slapped a hand to one ear. The voice seemed to be coming from inside her head. She stared at the spider, astonished, and noticed the two boys gaping as well.

"Now, Arachnea," said the old man, soothing his companion with a gentle finger. "Don't be offended. This girl is actually a great admirer of spiders. But remember, you are unique. Why wouldn't she question what she's seeing?"

"*An admirer. Is that true, girl?*"

"Yes," said Jori reluctantly, trying to figure out how and why she was having a conversation with a spider. "It is."

"Interesting. Spider-human interaction has traditionally not been pleasant, often concluding with a nasty smear on a wall."

"I wouldn't do that." Intrigued despite herself, Jori held out her hand, close to the old man's shoulder. Arachnea hesitated, then skittered forward and jumped onto Jori's open palm, her six glittering eyes fixed on Jori's two.

"No revulsion. No fear. I find this quite fascinating."

Derek winced as the spider began creeping up Jori's arm. "You're are a freak, you know that, Jori? You're a real freak."

"Yeah," she said, turning the scarred side of her face toward Derek. "So I've been told."

Newt's gaze kept shifting from the spider to the tapestry. "So how does it work?" he asked the old man. His face was tight, impatient.

"Allow us to demonstrate. Arachnea? If you would be so kind."

Arachnea scurried back down Jori's arm, onto the old man's outstretched palm. He walked toward the tapestry and raised his hand to the faded area he had pointed out earlier. The spider scuttled onto the empty stretch of fabric.

Mr. DePris reached again for the velvet pouch he had used around the fire, and carefully poured some of the colored crystals into his right palm. Raising his hand to his lips, he blew gently, sending a sparkling cloud into the air and onto the spider, who waited, tense and eager.

"Now then," said the old man. "Who would like to be first?"

An alarm sounded in Jori's head. But Newt almost jumped toward the old man.

"I would," he said. "I'll try it."

"Wonderful. Yours was an absolutely splendid dream. And I wonder . . . did you also bring something with you today, as I had asked? It might prove useful now."

Newt pulled the DVD out of his pocket. The old man gazed at it for a moment, held it in front of Arachnea, and then passed his hand over Newt's eyes. "Sleep, my boy." Newt's eyelids drooped, and he blinked twice. Then his chin settled against his chest, and his eyes closed completely.

Derek's smirk began to fade. "What did you just do? Hypnosis?"

"Oh, no," said the old man. "This is so much more." He leaned toward Newt and began to whisper. "All right, my friend. Find once more the dream you wove around the fire. It should still be quite close, hovering in the twilight of your mind. Do you see it?" Newt nodded. "Then go." Newt stood motionless for a moment, then sank slowly to the ground.

The old man waited until Newt's breathing became slower, deeper. "Arachnea, my dear. Are you ready?"

"*Of course.*" Jori looked toward the tapestry and saw a long, shining thread stream from Arachnea's abdomen and float out into the air. When it reached the point just over Newt's head, it twitched and hesitated.

A moment later, the thread started to divide, splitting itself into smaller and smaller tendrils that wove themselves into a delicate web of light. The web sparked and crackled, then drifted downward over Newt, capturing him in its glimmering strands.

He sighed, relaxing into an even deeper sleep. With every breath he took, the threads glowed more intensely, each taking on a different hue until the web seemed spun of stained glass. The strands began to pulse, and the colors flowed like tiny rivers back toward the tapestry. Toward Arachnea.

The spider stood absolutely still, waiting patiently as the brilliant hues spilled into her abdomen, where they shimmered and swirled.

"What's happening?" Jori whispered, torn between fascination and fear.

Mr. DePris placed a soothing hand on her shoulder. "Don't be alarmed, my dear. What you're seeing are simply the colors of your friend's dream, released from his mind and flowing from his heart. It's a sight that never ceases to enchant me."

The stream of colors slowed, then finally disappeared entirely from the web. Arachnea detached herself from the strand and anchored it securely. Next, she turned, extended her spinnerets, and exploded into motion.

New strands of silk began to spool from her, all in the dream-colors that had poured from Newt's mind. As each strand appeared, Arachnea wove it into the empty fabric on the tapestry. Within minutes, a village formed, and trees, and tiny figures on a hillside.

Jori took a step toward the picture but was pushed aside by Derek, who scanned the scene eagerly. His eyes narrowed. "Something's wrong," he said. "These ones aren't moving."

"Of course not," replied the old man. "Dreams can't live without their dreamer." He turned back to the tapestry. "Arachnea, my pet, you have outdone yourself. Now. Would you please allow our friend Nathaniel to see what you have created for him?"

"*Certainly.*" Arachnea retrieved Newt's dream strand from where she had anchored it, then centered it in the newly-spun village. The strand glowed once more, and the web covering Newt began beating like a heart. Jori began to tremble, certain that Newt himself was growing fainter.

Her eyes traveled the length of the dream strand to where it met the tapestry. At that exact spot, a tiny figure was forming. A thin, long-limbed boy with dirty-blond hair, sitting huddled on the ground.

"No," she whispered.

"What?" asked Derek. "What's going on?"

Jori pointed, and Derek's jaw dropped.

As they watched, the figure formed fully and raised his head. When he did, the images in the picture quivered to life. Men on horseback galloped into the village, their faces urgent. Others ran out to meet them, gesturing wildly, as women and children hurried toward the safety of their huts. The boy in the picture stood up slowly, looking around in amazement.

"No way," said Derek quietly.

"Oh, yes," chuckled the old man. "Very definitely." His eyes were sparkling. "Even as we stand here, your friend is living his dream, beginning an adventure he could only imagine before."

Derek spun away from the tapestry, all attitude gone. His eyes locked onto the old man's. "I need to go in, too."

"Why, of course. I wouldn't have brought you here, otherwise. And then Jori can have her turn."

Jori's palms grew moist. "No thanks," she said, fingering the small silver wolf she'd brought in her pocket. "I'll just watch, for now."

But Derek almost leaped toward the tapestry. He pulled a crumpled scrap of paper from inside his jacket—something torn from a book or magazine, Jori thought— and showed it quickly to the old man. "Let's do it."

Mr. DePris passed his hand in front of Derek's face. His eyes closed immediately, and, like Newt, he sank to the ground. Once again, Arachnea began to spin and gather and weave her threads.

Within minutes, a land of red rock and sand dunes had formed, and then a contrasting stretch of soft gold, deep jade, and sea-slate blue. In that section, a small city began to grow, fanning out from the waters to where a white marble building sat atop a high hill. Who'd have expected this? Jori thought, surprised. Then she watched, alarmed and envious, as Derek entered a world of his own imagining.

The old man turned to her, eyes smiling. "Go on, my dear. You know how much you want to."

Jori didn't answer. He bent toward her and put a hand on her cheek.

"Dear girl. Don't be afraid. After all, what are dreams, really? Nothing more than memories, hopes, desires. Regrets pulled through the prism of the mind and made beautiful."

Listening to his hypnotic voice, Jori allowed her heart to remember, just for a moment. She thought of her father, her sister, and the secret valley she had shared with them every night, so long ago. Each so precious, and each so very lost— part of her life now only when she slept.

"Okay," she whispered. "Okay."

Hearing her, Arachnea sprang into position on the tapestry. Jori stepped in front of Mr. DePris and nervously pressed the miniature wolf into his palm. He studied it, then looked at her affectionately. "Sleep, my dear."

Almost immediately, Jori's knees grew weak, and she sank to the floor. She saw the jeweled dust float from the old man's palm, and soon the light strands of Arachnea's web settled over her, warming her.

Contentment swirled through her. In her mind, the green forest and amber field took shape, etched against flashing peaks of crystal and light. But she was not yet willing to surrender herself completely, and strained to hear the voices around her.

"Beautiful," murmured the old man. "Just beautiful."

"It is. But then, when has my weaving not been beautiful?"

"Truly spoken, my dear."

"*Still, Jonas, it will almost be a pity to make this one live. The girl has more to commend her than most.*"

"Sympathizing with our prey, Arachnea? How out of character."

Jori's skin turned to ice, and she forced her eyes open.

Something was wrong. The old man's face looked darker, somehow, his limbs longer. And his smile . . . his smile seemed so cold.

A nervous whimper escaped her, and the old man's head snapped around. She quickly closed her eyes, feigning sleep. Just then, Arachnea's voice buzzed in her head. "*Interesting. This image is almost identical to another one . . . .*"

"Hush, Arachnea," said the old man. "Concentrate on your work."

"*But I've never seen this before. Two different dreams, but as similar as—*"

"I said that's enough!" the old man hissed, whipping his cane against the tapestry. Startled, both Jori and Arachnea jumped. The spider dropped the dream strand, and Jori, now wide awake, scraped the web from her face and clothes. She leaped to her feet, shaking, searching frantically for Newt. Both he and Derek still slept under their shimmering webs, as still as stone.

"Bring them out now," she whispered. "Please, bring them out."

Mr. DePris rushed over to her, the shadows gone. "Oh, my dear girl. What's wrong? You seem distressed."

"Just get them out of there. Please."

"But they're having a delightful time. Just as you will, when you—"

"No!" Jori shouted. Her voice dropped back to a whisper. "What are you doing to us?"

"I don't understand."

"Yes, you do."

He sighed. "Perhaps I do. Sometimes a dreamer is caught between worlds, seeing neither clearly. That must have happened in your case, my dear. Still, I would not for one moment cause you any concern. I'll bring your friends back immediately. Would that reassure you?"

Jori nodded, still trembling.

The old man touched her cheek, then stepped over the sleeping forms of the two boys and ran his hand backward along their dream strands. At his touch, the webs once again began to glow.

Newt and Derek began to twitch and mutter on the floor. Their faint forms became more substantial, taking back life and color from the strands that enmeshed them. Within moments, the webs faded from their bodies.

"You see," said the old man. "Nothing whatsoever to worry about."

The boys sat up slowly, looking dazed. "Well, my friends?" said Mr. DePris. "What do you think of my 'rug' now?"

Newt shook his head, and Jori watched his eyes dart over invisible images. "It was . . . amazing. Like being in a movie, or living every dream I ever had." His eyes locked onto Jori's and he leaped to his feet, grabbing her by the shoulders. His hands were shaking. "Can you believe this?"

Derek was muttering to himself, raking his fingers through his hair. He looked up at the old man, his face feverish. "Why'd you bring us back so fast? I wasn't ready yet."

Jori started to speak, but Mr.DePris answered more quickly. "Simply to make sure you weren't disappointed."

Derek nodded, but seemed barely to be listening. "Listen. I gotta go out for a few minutes. I gotta get . . . to take care of something." He ran toward the door, then paused, looking back at the old man. "Okay if I come back later?"

"Of course."

"Thanks." Derek bolted out of the tapestry room and Jori listened to his feet pound down the stairs. She heard a surprised bark from Gopher, a short laugh, and then the sound of the front door slamming.

"Derek said 'thanks,'" Jori said, amazed.

"There," the old man said to her, eyes twinkling. "You see? He was obviously quite pleased with his little adventure. Now, why don't you two wait for me downstairs? I'll be along momentarily."

He walked over to the tapestry and patted his pocket. But Arachnea scuttled away from him, up to a dark corner of the ceiling. Her voice scratched at the edge of Jori's mind, barely audible, and she hung back to listen.

"How dare you treat me like that!" the spider hissed. *"Whipping your cane at me."*

"Arachnea—"

"Especially considering you'd have nothing, be nothing, without me. Just an old man with a bag of sand."

"Never assume, my pet. You're valuable, yes. But not indispensable." He looked at the spider thoughtfully, one finger tapping his lips.

Jori hurried after Newt, who had already wandered past the red door, still looking dazed. A few of the floorboards melted away, revealing the staircase.

As they descended, Newt suddenly began to talk nonstop, gesturing wildly as he described what he'd done on his brief journey into the tapestry. Then he paused in midsentence.

"Hey, I haven't let you say anything. So, come on, tell me what you saw." His face was eager, as though he needed her dreams as well as his own.

Jori shrugged, embarrassed. "I didn't see anything."

"What do you mean? Didn't it work for you?"

"No. I mean I didn't go in."

"You didn't . . ." Jori felt his disappointment hanging between them. "Why not?"

"It's hard to explain. Things I thought I saw. And heard."

"Like what?"

Jori glanced behind, making sure Mr. DePris had not yet appeared. She grabbed Newt's hand, pulling him down the last few steps. "Listen, Newt. We've got to get out of here. Something's not right. With the old man. With the tapestry. Everything."

Newt shifted uncomfortably. "What are you talking about?"

"Oh, come on. A talking spider, magic furniture. That little trip you just took through the web. Either the old man is doing something to our heads, or this house is part of the *Twilight Zone*."

Newt turned on her angrily. "If something's not right here, it's you. This place is amazing. Or are you just too warped and paranoid to enjoy anything anymore?"

Jori was startled into speechlessness. Newt continued to glare at her, but then blinked in surprise.

"Sorry," he muttered. "I don't know why I said that."

"You okay? "

He looked away. "Yeah, sure."

Mr. DePris appeared above them. "Is something the matter?"

"No," said Newt, looking back at Jori, almost daring her to speak. "Everything's great."

The old man smiled serenely and started down the stairs. Newt's expression relaxed.

"That was really terrific up there, " he said. "Thanks for showing us."

"Oh, my boy, it was truly my pleasure." The old man's eyes slid over to Jori. "And perhaps next time, Jori will be able to enjoy it as well."

"Yeah," said Newt, a slight edge to his voice. "That would be nice, wouldn't it?"

Tension buzzed beneath Jori's skin. She was the odd one out, the only person not enthralled by whatever was going on in this house. She moved awkwardly toward the shelves and display cases, her eyes skimming the contents for any distraction.

She gasped, clutching at the edge of a chair.

On one shelf, so high up she had almost missed it, sat a winged unicorn. And a glass globe in which liquid rainbow colors swirled like clouds.

"Where did you get those?" she whispered.

"Get what, my dear?"

"Those. The unicorn. And the globe."

He moved next to her, peering up at the objects. "I'm sorry. I'm not certain I recall."

Jori's stared directly into his eyes. "They belong to my sister."

"Really!" The old man looked astonished. "How strange. Well, if that's true, you must take them home to her."

"She's not *at* home. And you know it." Jori began to back away. "So tell me. Why did you keep her things? As souvenirs? *Trophies?*"

Newt grabbed her by the arm. "Stop it, Jori. You don't think—"

"I don't know what to think. But I'm leaving."

Newt's face twisted with anger. "Fine. Go ahead."

Jori swallowed, her growing horror battling with concern for Newt. "Come on, Newt. Please. Let's get out of here."

Newt turned away and crossed to the fire. He stared into the flames.

Mr. DePris's eyes narrowed. "Apparently, my dear, you aren't quite persuasive enough."

Jori began to edge toward the door. The old man followed her.

"What a dark little mind you have," he said. "Suspicious of me, afraid of my tapestry. What could be wrong with something that erases pain and eases the yearnings of the heart?"

Jori didn't answer, only knew she wanted desperately to escape the house, to run from the old man and whatever was upstairs. Because now she could see something new in his eyes.

Hunger.

"Of course," he said, his words like hot needles, "if you prefer the other world, you may return to it. Find out, my dear, what it has to teach you. You had one lesson, when your father died. When he gave you those scars. But there is so much more to learn. Watch as winter kills the gardens and freezes the homeless you pass by each day. Watch as that mother you love grows old and tired, worn down by grief and despair. Watch yourself become lost and bitter, friendless and frightened."

He leaned closer, whispering now. "But remember. Only return to me and touch a jeweled thread, and the ugliness disappears."

Jori's hand finally found the door. Flinging it open, she lurched outside and scrambled through the garden, stumbling over roots and stones that thrust themselves in her way. She shoved her way past the garden door and tore into the alley, away from the glowing yard. And as she ran, she held her hands over her ears to shut out the old man's hideous, mocking laughter.

EIGHT

VANISHED

Two days later, Jori sat stiffly in detention hall, willing Newt to walk through the door. He hadn't shown up on Thursday, either. When she'd checked with Mr. Alvarez, he told her that Newt had been marked with an unexcused absence for the entire day. "Which means I'll be seeing him here next week, too," the little man said, tapping his attendance sheet with satisfaction.

Jori was in an agony of confusion. The moment she'd returned home on the day she escaped from the old man, she'd called her mother to tell her what had happened—at least, as much as she could explain without sounding crazy. Within a few hours, two police officers had been dispatched to the Bridgeview area to investigate.

Jori and her mother huddled on the couch all evening, gripping each other's hands until their fingers were white. Around 10:30 the phone finally rang. Jori's mom leaped for the receiver, her face wild with hope. But as she listened, the hope drained away. Jori didn't like what replaced it.

Her mother fumbled the phone back into its cradle. She said nothing for a few moments, but her face was pale, her eyes frightened.

"What is it?" Jori asked, heart thumping. "What did they find?"

"Nothing. They didn't find anything, Jori."

Jori stared, stunned. Her mom sat down next to her, taking both of Jori's hands in hers.

"They followed your directions, but all they found was an abandoned building. They said it matched your description—at least a little. There was a wall. And a garden, or what's left of one. But no one lives there. No one has for years."

Jori's mind swam. Either the house off Bridgeview hid a horror worse than she suspected, or something was very, very wrong with her. Her mom's arm slipped around her shoulders, and Jori felt a soft kiss on her forehead.

"You know, sweetie, sometimes worry and stress can build up over months, without us even knowing it. The detective said that maybe . . . maybe you're more exhausted or unhappy than either of us has realized. That maybe we need to talk to someone. What do you think?"

Jori felt all emotion drain from her. Then she simply nodded.

★ ★ ★

That had been Wednesday. When Newt didn't show up for school on Thursday, the emptiness inside Jori slowly changed to a dull ache of fear. And now, as she watched Mr. Alvarez smugly check off Newt's name for the second time, she became increasingly certain that she hadn't imagined the old man, the house, or what happened on the second floor.

She began to doodle nervously on the cover of her binder, trying to release the tension burning along every nerve. First, she wrote Newt's name, touching it worriedly with her finger. Then she drew an old house, and a large spider dangling from an elaborate web. Finally, furiously, she pressed down on her pen and wrote DEPRIS, tracing the name over and over until it glared from the notebook in angry black letters.

She stared at the name in frustration, and at the pictures next to it. Her eyes widened.

It couldn't be.

She ripped a piece of paper from the binder, wrote the letter *S* on it, and crossed out that letter in the name of the old man. She did the same with the letter *P*. Then *I*. And continued until a single word crawled across the paper:

SPIDER

Jori leaped from her seat and stumbled toward the door. Mr. Alvarez's head snapped up from his mound of papers.

"Where do you think you're going?"

"Out."

"I don't think so." He stood and leaned across the metal desk. "Get back in your seat. And I mean now."

"I can't. I've got to go."

"Take one more step, young lady, and you'll be back here next week—with your friend Newt."

Jori's froze in the doorway at the sound of Newt's name. Oh God, she thought. I hope so.

She turned back toward the furious little man, whose scalp was now covered with large red blotches. "Listen, Mr. Alvarez. I need you to do something. Call my mom later. Tell her not to worry. Okay?"

Confusion replaced the anger on Mr. Alvarez's face. "What do you mean? Why can't you call her yourself?"

"Just do it, okay?"

"Wait, Jori. Please. Tell me—"

But she was out the door.

★ ★ ★

Fifteen minutes later, Jori reached Bridgeview, still trying to pull together her tattered thoughts. How could she have been so stupid? The old man had practically told them what was going on. He was a collector, all right, like any other spider. But the victims he preyed on were human.

New fears gnawed at her. She had escaped, but what about those who hadn't? Newt, her sister. The others whose dreams still swirled in the tapestry. Would the old man just suck them dry of their fantasies, then discard what was left? Her mind conjured a vision of the monster crouching low over a pale human form, leaning toward it, open mouthed. Her legs weakened, and she leaned against a signpost for support.

Then, like a lifeline, the professor's own words unraveled from her memory: *Dreams can't live without their dreamers*, he'd said.

Jori nodded fiercely. "You haven't won yet, old man."

She sprinted through the sidestreets, past the broken street lamps and into the dark alleys. When she neared the final passageway, she slowed and crept toward it, watching for the soft glow of the garden.

It never came.

Cautiously, Jori eased herself around the corner. She gasped.

It was all gone. Well, not gone, exactly. A building stood at the end of the street, but it wasn't the one she had visited three times before. This was an ordinary two-flat, its roof sagging, its walls crumbling. The stone wall that once hid it from view had all but collapsed, and the towering oaks were leafless, riddled with disease, the bare bones of their branches clawing at the sky.

No wonder the police thought she was nuts. Jori walked toward the garden door, now a dull, weathered gray. Its rusted metal socket stared at her blindly, the glass orb gone. Jori took a deep breath and grasped the brass knob.

It came off in her hand.

She looked blankly at the handle, then dropped it on the broken concrete. Tentatively, she pushed on the door itself. With a groan of splintering wood, it collapsed halfway into the yard, caught at the last moment by the lower of its two broken hinges. Jori walked over it as though it were a drawbridge, looking around in shock.

The garden was dead, its blankets of flowers now rotting mats of stems and leaves. A septic stench rose from them, and Jori retched, her stomach heaving. The vines that had cascaded from the trees now hung like frayed ropes from dead limbs, casting gallows-like shadows across the yard.

Jori gazed at it all in bewilderment. But then she knew.

It's always been like this, she thought. We only thought we saw the door, the cottage . . . the Moon Garden. The old man got into our heads before we even met him.

And now there was no longer any need for tempting façades. The spider had what he wanted.

The thought jolted Jori from her daze. She crouched, fingers touching the ground, and slowly duckwalked through the swaying weeds that swallowed the yard. Their cold stems sliced at her hands and cheeks.

The front door creaked, and Jori fell flat. Someone was creeping through the grass, pausing every few steps as though looking for something. Looking for her? Her insides twisted. A moment later, she heard harsh breathing above her, and something cold touched her face. She yelped, striking out with one arm.

"Bwoof?"

Jori jerked up, and Gopher scrambled backwards.

Laughing softly, she reached out to pat the big dog's head. But her hand froze halfway there. The dog was little more than raw, red skin stretched over bone. His eyes were sunken, his back covered with running sores.

"Poor Gopher," Jori whispered. "Is this how he really treats you?" The dog whined. She rummaged quickly through her pockets and held out the remains of a power bar. Gopher swallowed it in one starving gulp.

"Gopher," she said, kneeling next to him and cradling his head. "I know what's happening in there. And if I can get the others out, I'll take care of you, too. I swear." The dog whimpered.

"Now," she said. "All I've got to do is find our charming old professor and figure out how to get past him." She laughed hopelessly. "Yeah, that's all." But Gopher's dull eyes had lit at the word "professor." Taking Jori's hand gently in his mouth, he pulled her toward one of the cracked, filthy windows at the side of the house. Slowly, she raised her head until her eyes were just past the sill.

There sat the old man, as unrecognizable as the house itself. His body was gaunt and twisted under threadbare clothes, and the skin of his face looked like scraps of tissue pasted to his skull. Eyes closed, he rocked back and forth in an ancient chair, sucking in air through rotted teeth.

Jori dropped back to the grass, skin crawling. She looked at the dog. "So now what do I do? How do I get upstairs without him seeing me?"

Gopher listened, his head tilted to one side. Then he stood, licked her hand, and hobbled to the front of the house.

Where he shrieked and howled as though he'd gone mad.

Jori's heart dropped. Was the starving dog just another of the old man's tricks, a ruse to draw her closer? She cowered against the wall as Gopher yelped and whined and cried. Then she heard a crash, followed by the tortured screech of the front door hinges.

"Shut up, you miserable mongrel!" the old man roared. But Gopher continued to yelp wildly, his barks echoing down the dark streets. Jori peered around the corner just as Mr. DePris lunged toward the dog, his cane raised over his head. "I said, shut up! Shut up or I'll crack your skull open!" Gopher growled, then leaped forward and buried his teeth in the old man's leg.

The professor howled, and his cane clattered to the ground. He clutched at his thigh, now black with blood, and screamed obscenities at the dog. Gopher stumbled backward and collapsed, his weak legs finally failing him. The old man looked up, grinned viciously, and grabbed once more for his cane.

"Turn on me, will you?" His lips curled back and he raised the cane, eyes hot with fury. But before he could strike, Gopher scrambled to his feet and hobbled frantically over the broken garden door, into the darkness of the alley.

Mr. DePris hesitated, turning to stare hungrily up at the second-floor window. But Gopher barked again, taunting him. The old man's red eyes narrowed, and he stalked angrily after the dog, his thin frame quickly swallowed by the shadows.

Jori darted around the side of the house and rushed through the doorway. She jerked to a stop, gagging.

It was as though a corpse, not a man, inhabited the house. The once comfortable room was now a pit of decay, stinking of rot and worms. Shredded cobwebs drooped in the corners, and the heavy oak furniture was warped and split. The torn upholstery of the old velvet furniture reeked of rodent droppings, and all the fine collections had vanished, or moldered under layers of dust.

Jori shook off her revulsion and raced to the staircase, taking the steps two at a time. She reached the second floor—no longer masked by the illusion of a ceiling—and strode to the one thing that was still beautiful: the shining door that guarded the tapestry room.

Jori pushed her way inside, ready to run to the tapestry. But she stopped when she saw what lay on the floor.

Beneath a dozen sparkling nets, human figures lay motionless. Some had all but disappeared. Others were little more than dried husks, ready to crumble into dust. Still others looked as though the dreamers had just curled up for a pleasant nap and would soon awaken. How had they all not seen this before?

But she knew, of course. They had seen only what the old man wanted them to see. A talking door. A magic cottage. An enchanted ceiling. Innocent images plucked from their memories, designed to delight them, to comfort them—to trap them.

She looked up at the tapestry, searching until she located Newt's village. Trembling, she followed his dream strand back into the room. He lay at the end of the thread, still as death, long hair covering his closed eyes.

"Newt, you idiot," she whispered. She reached over to touch his shoulder, but the net that covered him crackled and burned.

A low voice pierced her mind.

"And what do you think you're doing?" Jori winced. *"Up here, human."*

Arachnea hung directly above her, rubbing her front legs together.

"I've come to get him out," said Jori, backing away from the spider. "Him . . . and someone else I think is lost in there."

"Out? What an interesting concept. No one has ever come out."

"Maybe that's because no one's ever tried to help them."

"True. But if some person were foolish enough to try—a silly young girl, for example—I might be forced to blind her, sting her, paralyze her, to keep her from doing harm to the tapestry."

"Interesting," said Jori, folding her arms. "Because that same person might be forced to defend herself by reducing a certain spider to one of those smears on the wall she once mentioned."

There was a brief silence, and the spider pulled herself further away from Jori. "You certainly are a most fascinating creature."

"You better believe it." Jori looked away from Arachnea, searching the shrouded shapes on the floor for one that might be Lisa. But too many of the forms had settled, shifted, faded to a point where their features were impossible to discern.

Except for one, much larger than the rest. Jori peered at it curiously and saw two dreamers captured under one sparkling web. One was a girl with wavy black hair. The other, a slim boy in a brown leather coat.

Derek and Marisa.

She followed their dream strand up to the tapestry, and was surprised to see it connected to the same broad expanse of dune and desert that Derek had first imagined. She could see little of the gleaming city, though—just blazing rock and white-gold sand that shimmered in the heat of an invisible sun.

Good, Jori thought. I hope you rot there.

She returned her attention to the spider. If she couldn't persuade the creature to help her, she wouldn't be saving anyone.

"Look, Arachnea," Jori said. "You don't have to worry. I don't want to wreck your tapestry. Or you."

"So you say."

"Well, I can guarantee I'm safer than your professor. Didn't he almost kill you the other day?"

The spider didn't answer.

"Come to think of it," she said, spinning a little deception of her own, "he told us that you'd been a bit of a problem lately, but that he was—'tolerating it,' I think he said—because soon he wouldn't need you anymore."

That did it. The spider's legs shot out stiffly, and she jerked up and down on her dragline in agitated spurts. *"I knew it! I knew it! The ingrate. After all this time . . . How dare he . . ."*

Jori let the creature rant. But then her nerves began singing, sensing the imminent return of the more dangerous human spider.

"Arachnea. I just need a little information from you, that's all. When you started weaving my dream, you said it was like another one in the tapestry. Can you show me?"

The spider's spasms stopped, followed by a few seconds of silence.

"Why not?" she said. *"You certainly seem more deserving of my help than he."*

She swung herself over to the tapestry, crawled across the shining threads. *"Here. This one."*

Jori almost shut her eyes, not sure she could bear to look. But there it was. A golden meadow. Blue velvet hills. And the towering crystal mountain.

She started to follow the glowing dream strand to the shape it drew life from, but then she stopped. If only a shell remained, she wasn't ready to know that. Not just yet.

She held out her palm, and the spider scuttled onto it.

"Arachnea, listen. This dream, it's my sister's. She's the one I want to bring back. Newt, too, if I can. Unless . . . it's already too late."

The spider seemed to consider. *"No. I don't believe it is. If the dreams are still vibrant in the tapestry, and if the dreamers are still visible out here, then I imagine they remain balanced between both worlds, and can choose to live in either."*

"But you said no one has ever come out."

"That's true. But perhaps they didn't realize they had to make the choice."

"They still don't know."

"No, they don't." Arachnea crawled forward, her six eyes glittering. *"But now you can tell them. You can go in after them."*

Jori stared. "Go in—how?"

"The same way the others did. The old man's dust almost coats the floor, easy enough to gather. So if you dream, I'll

spin. In fact—" She hopped back onto the gleaming image of Lisa's dreamscape, *"since you and your sister shared a similar vision, I can weave your dream into hers."*

"What about Newt?"

"His dreamscape is quite close to hers. Perhaps you'll be able to move between them."

Jori's mind was whirling, but Arachnea was making a strange kind of sense. "So say this works, and I find them. How do I—we—get out again?"

"Simply anchor your dream strand where you'll be able to locate it again. I'll make new links out here, and you can all use the same way out."

Jori leaned in toward the spider. "Thank you, Arachnea."

"You're welcome, human." The spider was silent for a moment. *"There's one piece of advice I'd like to give you, though. Try not to stay too long."*

"I don't plan to. But why?"

"Look again at the tapestry. Where it's dark."

Jori looked. For the first time, she noticed an irregular black stain throbbing at the center. Within it, shapes gave way to shadows, and dark forms slithered through an unseen landscape. Seeping out from the darkness, crawling into the faded sections of the tapestry, were thick black lines that flowed like rivers.

"What is that?" she whispered.

"I don't know. I didn't weave it. It simply appeared one day. But it grows every time another dream starts dying."

Even as Arachnea spoke, a black tentacle squirmed from the center of the tapestry, snaking between the sparkling images. It reached a magnificent dreamscape of an African veldt and bit into it. The image immediately began to throb, the colors draining from it.

Jori looked away before she could consider the meaning of what she was seeing. She sat on the floor and closed her eyes. "Okay, Arachnea. Let's do this fast, before the old man comes back." She blew out her breath nervously. "And before I change my mind."

"All right. If you're sure." The spider's voice was oddly subdued. *"Good luck, human."*

Jori could barely think above the blood pounding in her ears. Finally, she shook her head and arms, forced her mind to clear. Just picture home, she told herself. Home the way it used to be. Mom and Dad are laughing in the kitchen, and I'm in my bed, remembering the story . . .

Her fear drifted away, and soon she felt the soft threads of Arachnea's web settle over her, warm as an embrace. Jori sighed, forgetting all about the decayed house, the black rivers, and the monster who would soon be coming up the stairs.

NINE

AVENDAR

Jori breathed deeply—more deeply than she had in months—and curled onto her side, content as a small child. She felt her body grow warm, weightless, each atom glowing with some strange energy. When no sense of her physical self remained, her spirit slipped gently from her body, into a halo of light.

A sapphire ribbon shimmered above her. My dream strand, Jori thought. As she watched, it drifted downward, wrapped itself around her, and began to pulse with the flickering images it drew from her mind. She became one with the dream, and together they rose into a silent sky. The room below became a distant miniature, then vanished completely.

In its place, an emerald field unfurled like a satin quilt. Within that field, familiar images took shape. Rolling blue hills. The golden meadow. And a midnight forest, darkly welcoming.

The strand widened, rippling like waves toward shore, and Jori took form again on its billowing surface. One wave, larger than the rest, lifted her onto its crest and carried her down toward the forest canopy. The branches of the tallest tree gathered her in, then passed her tenderly from bough to bough. Within moments, the gentle swinging motion lulled her into a deep, dreamless sleep.

Hours later, Jori woke to the splendor of a full moon, her head cushioned on a soft pillow of moss and leaves. A cool breeze played across her face, and she breathed in the fragrance of resin and honey. In the moonlight, the glen gleamed as though dusted with memories.

Sitting up, Jori stretched her arms and arched her back in a cat-like awakening. As she did, her fingers touched a bright blue thread that dangled just a few inches away, suspended from nothing.

The dream strand, Jori realized. She closed her fingers around it, and noticed that her hand was still tight with scar tissue. Good, she thought grimly. I still know what I am and where I am.

As if to underscore the thought, a long howl sounded in the distance.

Jori stood and surveyed the glen, trying to locate some safe landmark that would allow her to find the strand again when the time came to leave. At the base of a nearby cliff, a ghostly white birch stood sentry. She moved to it and bent down, winding the blue thread carefully around the base of its trunk.

The howl cut through the air again, and Jori stiffened. It hadn't sounded so close, before. The piercing note rang a third time, now rising from just beyond the ring of trees. Other voices joined in, their harsh cries blending into a chilling chorus that grew louder and wilder with each call. Jori's breath came faster. *Whatever they are*, she thought, *they have my scent. And they're everywhere.*

Then suddenly, terribly, the howling stopped. From all around the clearing, yellow eyes reflected the moonlight. Jori trembled as dark shapes formed behind those eyes— shapes with massive chests, pointed ears, and teeth like sharpened spikes.

Wolves.

She felt her palms grow moist. It was one thing to collect figures on a shelf, another entirely to hear the harsh growls of a pack, sense the wild heat of their bodies. As though smelling her fear, the animals crept from the darkness and formed a half-circle around her, gray coats edged with moonglow. Jori backed herself against the face of the rock, next to the swaying birch. She crouched and felt blindly for the dream strand. But her hand was shaking too much to find it.

One of the largest beasts broke from the circle and stalked over to her. He sniffed her neck and arms, then gazed steadily into her eyes. Satisfied, he turned back to his companions. Jori blinked, certain she'd seen him nod.

At his signal, the wolves sat back on their haunches and threw back their heads. Once more, their howls shattered the silence. The moon gleamed brighter, as though drawing energy from their wild keening.

Jori listened, terrified and awestruck. Then a high, clear note sounded above her, so pure and piercing that it drowned out the harsher voices of the wolves. Their howls trailed off and they drew together, facing the wall of rock. Golden eyes gleaming, they stretched their front legs in a stiff-legged bow.

The powerful note ended in a guttural growl. To Jori's surprise, someone spoke from just overhead, the voice as deep and primal as the forest itself.

"You have done well, my friends."

Jori's heart leaped. There was someone here, then, someone who could rescue her from this deadly circle of wolves.

"Hey!" she shouted. "I need some help! I don't know how long I've got until these things decide I'm dinner."

There was no answer. But a bolt of energy streaked through the air, exploding in the clearing like a new-made star. Jori gasped as a magnificent silver she-wolf leaped from the nimbus of light and wheeled around to face her. The wolf's eyes flashed with a startling intelligence, and her coat shone more brightly than the moon.

"Welcome, girl," she said.

Jori stared. "Who are you?"

"My name is Ragar. And this is Avendar."

For just a moment, the memory of her father's story ached inside her: *In the greenest of the green forests of Avendar, there lived a lone wolf . . .*

"Yes," said the wolf, as though reading her mind. "And so you know that you have nothing to fear from me." Jori said nothing, still wary of the beasts that ringed her in. Ragar's eyes flashed with amusement. "And no one here is planning to eat you, either."

"You sure about that?"

Ragar's jaws parted in a canine grin. But she growled low in her throat, and her companions melted into the forest. Jori's shoulders relaxed. The silver wolf continued.

"It is good that you have come, and good that you arrived on the first night of the full moon. We might not have found you, otherwise."

"You were looking for me?"

"Of course. From the moment I sensed you were here."

"And why was that, exactly?"

"To watch over you. To offer my help, when and if it is needed."

She's not real, Jori reminded herself. She comes out of my own head. "I don't need any help. Especially not from a figment."

Ragar was silent for a moment. "Your mind is more powerful than anything else in this world, girl. Don't dismiss what it offers you—no matter how unlikely the form." Her dark eyes were now cool, measuring. "And remember this, as well. Confidence is a fine trait. But arrogance is something else entirely."

Jori's face burned. But then she weighed what the wolf was telling her. To survive in the tapestry, in this mind-world, she'd have to refrain from her customary cynicism, and her even more customary stubbornness. She forced a respectful tone into her voice.

"All right. I'm sorry, Ragar. And I do need your help."

"I know. Come with me." The wolf walked to the edge of the clearing and disappeared down a rough path. Jori hurried after her, following the faint silver glow as the wolf slipped ghostlike through the woods. She could hear the rest of the pack shadowing them, nearby but unseen.

After a mile or so, the forest began to thin, and dawn parted the shifting green canopy. Flashes of colored light vibrated on the stones and tree trunks, and Jori walked more quickly, knowing the likely source. She raced toward the edge of the forest and broke through the last stand of trees, heart pounding.

Yes, she thought. Yes.

The golden meadow stretched before her, its feather-tipped grasses rippling in a warm breeze. Pink shrubs scented the air with peppermint, and tiny winged creatures with dragon-like bodies darted from blossom to blossom.

And shining like a gift, miles in the distance, the Crystal Mountain soared into the sky, reaching through a halo of clouds to capture the full glory of sunrise. Bright rays poured through the glass cliffs, sending a thousand rainbows to dance over all of Avendar.

Jori leaped into the sea of meadow grasses. She breathed deeply of the candy-scented air, stared at pastel clouds pinwheeling overhead, reached for the corkscrew branches winding out from the trees. Then, arms outstretched and eyes closed, she began to run, imagining her fingertips brushing those of her sister, allowing herself, just for a moment, to believe the feeling was real.

Soon, she thought, losing herself in the dream. Maybe this all will be over soon, and Mom won't have to pretend anymore . . .

She reached the base of the blue hills and began to climb, Ragar pacing steadily at her side. About halfway up, Jori looked to her left, and her steps slowed. A mile or two in the distance, the soothing colors of Avendar ended abruptly, as though hacked off with a jagged knife. Along the raw edge of earth, a seething black river thrashed against its banks as though trying to escape.

Jori remembered the tapestry, saw again the black tentacles squirming from its center. Her small flame of hope began to flicker.

"What is that?" Jori asked, although she already knew.

Ragar stared at the wild water, the skin pulling back from her teeth. "That is the Black River. It is a diseased thing. Insane."

A low moan drifted toward them from the water, spiking into a furious howl.

Jori looked at Ragar, trembling.

"And that is the voice of the river," the wolf said. "It is hungry today."

Jori pulled her eyes away from the churning water, tried to block out the sound of its screams. She raced to the crest of the hill, desperate to soothe her eyes with a glimpse of her sister's valley. She clambered to the very top—and stopped, horrified.

The valley was dying.

Nothing green remained, no flowers bloomed. The bright river that had once meandered across the valley floor had shrunken to a clotted artery of mud. A ghastly yellow haze hung over the entire landscape, warping the weak light that struggled through it. And trapped in its sickly glow, like insects encased in amber, were the unicorns.

Some lay panting in the feeble light, eyes sunken, ribs heaving under dull hides. Others staggered toward what little remained of the stream, the silver light of their horns extinguished. And there were some, stretched out on the grass, that no longer moved at all.

"Ragar," whispered Jori. "What's happened to them?"

The wolf's eyes blazed. "Look at the mountain."

Jori raised her head. Although the topmost peaks of the Crystal Mountain still reached desperately toward the sun, the lower cliffs were dull and damaged. A dark mist swirled within them, leaking out through fissures in the glass, emitting the deadly yellow gas that suffocated the valley.

"But how?" Jori whispered. "Lisa wouldn't want this. She wouldn't let it happen."

"No? Remember, girl, that dark things crouch in the corners of your mind, things you aren't aware exist. And so even the gentlest dream can mask a nightmare."

Jori felt numb inside. If the dream was damaged—if it was dying—then what was happening to Lisa? She stumbled down the hill, Ragar at her heels, and fell to her knees next to one of the fallen unicorns. Cradling its head in her arms, she stroked it gently. But it was covered with sweat, its skin cold. The fever-ravaged eyes rolled toward her.

"You've come back."

The statement startled her. But then she understood. "No. That was my sister." Her heart beat faster. "Do you know where she is?"

But the beast could no longer speak.

Jori held him until his tortured breathing stopped, and a sob broke from her. Then a startled whinny pealed out on her right. A small group of unicorns huddled in a portion of the valley still warmed by the mountain's topmost peaks. Jori gently lowered the dead unicorn's head and hurried toward them.

She stopped just a few feet away, not sure what to say or do. One of the unicorns took a step toward her.

"Help us, please," it said, its voice a whisper. "Heal the mountain."

"Heal the—" She shrank from the desperation in his eyes. "I'm sorry. I don't know how."

"But you must know. You are so like the other. And the mountain sickened only when she did."

Jori's throat tightened.

"What do you mean, sickened? Tell me what happened."

The animals looked at each other in confusion, but then a second unicorn stepped forward.

"The girl was like you, but she was here from the moment any of us had a memory. We thought she must be the spirit of the mountain—she sparkled just as brightly."

Lisa's laughter rippled in Jori's mind, and her throat tightened.

"But then," said the first unicorn, "she began to grow restless, unhappy. And the more unhappy she became, the thinner and weaker she grew, and the more the shadows ate at the crystal."

"But what changed? What hurt her so badly?"

"We don't know. We tried to soothe her, but she became angry. She said we were tricking her, making her forget what she was really looking for. Not long after that, she disappeared."

Jori clenched her fists. God, Lisa. Even this wasn't enough?

"Do any of you know what she meant? What she wanted to find?"

"She never told us."

"Then think!" Jori said, stamping a foot. "One of you *has* to know something!"

A wild cry sliced through the poisoned air. Looking up, Jori saw a magnificent horned beast standing on the uppermost peak of the Crystal Mountain. The moment her gaze touched him, he began to leap down the mountainside.

"Who is that?" she asked.

One of the unicorns looked up, trembling. "Angel."

The huge unicorn jumped to the last of sparkling peaks, just above the cliffs where the black mist swirled. He reared up on his hind legs, screamed, and leaped from the edge, plummeting toward the riverbed.

Jori gasped. Then two magnificent white wings flared open on the unicorn's back and he took flight, soaring over the valley, riding the windstreams like an eagle. His powerful wings beat the air, lifted him higher and higher until Jori could barely see his silhouette against the sun. A moment later, he began spiraling downward, gliding toward the hill on which she stood.

Now his wings began to beat again, more gently this time, and he lowered himself soundlessly to the ground.

"Jori," he said. "I hoped you would find your way here."

She gaped at him. But at her side, Ragar nodded gravely, and the unicorn dipped his head respectfully in the wolf's direction. Jori finally found her voice.

"How do you know who I am? I don't remember you from . . . anywhere."

"Hair red as fire, a temper to match—I couldn't help but know you," Angel said, his eyes smiling. Then his voice grew softer. "Because I knew your sister well when she was here."

Jori felt a surge of relief. "So you must know why she left, where she was going. She must have told you."

"No. She disappeared without warning."

Frustration surged through her. "Then I guess you didn't know her as well as you thought."

Ragar growled disapprovingly, and Angel's eyes flashed, his wings stiffening at his sides.

"I knew her, girl, perhaps better than you. When she left, I felt as though my soul and body had been ripped apart!"

Jori flinched at the raw pain in his voice. "I'm sorry," she muttered. "Sometimes I say things without letting my brain check them out first."

Angel relaxed. "I know. It's all right."

"Still . . . don't you have any idea where she is?"

"I searched all of Avendar, but found no trace of her." Angel's eyes grew dark. "Which means yes, I do think I know where she is."

"Where?"

"Maligor."

Jori felt fear knife through her. She looked at Ragar.

"Maligor is the dark land, Jori," said the wolf. "It's where the Black Rivers come from, and where they all return."

The dark land. Once again, Jori pictured the throbbing heart of the old man's tapestry, heard the screams from the Black River. Then she remembered something Arachnea had said about the dark stain that had damaged her precious masterpiece: *It grows every time another dream starts dying.* And now Jori knew why. It swallowed the dreamers whose fantasies had betrayed them.

Jori sank to the ground, tears streaming down her face. "So that's it? She's gone forever?"

Angel glanced at Ragar. "Only if you want her to be."

"What? Of course I don't want her to be. What a stupid thing to say!"

The unicorn flexed his wings, but this time showed no anger. "Then you must go after her."

"No!" said one of the other unicorns, thrusting himself between Jori and Angel. "We need her here. If she goes, the mountain will die. We'll all die."

"Stay with us," the second unicorn pleaded. "We can protect you from the River. From the dark place."

Angel reared up and turned on them, lashing out with his hooves.

"Protect her!" he said in disgust, his eyes blazing. "I thought I could protect her sister. But I was wrong." Jori could hear the anguish in his voice. "Do you really think she'll be safe here? Or will she just lose her soul one morning and wander off, like the other did?"

The two unicorns cringed and retreated. Angel tossed his mane, then turned his attention back to Jori, who was trembling.

"The River didn't take your sister, Jori. She left on her own. A terrible thing, but at least it means she was still strong enough to choose her own path. And perhaps she is still strong enough to choose another, if someone were to help her."

"I want to help her. God, so much. But won't Maligor destroy me, too?"

"No," said Angel gently. "Not you. "

Jori turned to the silver wolf. "Ragar? What should I do?"

"You already know. You have no choice."

"No. I suppose I don't." But she hesitated, one detail not quite making sense. "Angel, if you knew where she was, why didn't you go after her?"

A shadow crossed Angel's face. "There were reasons."

Jori waited for him to say more, but he remained silent. "All right," she said finally. "I guess I'm going. But how do I get there? How do I cross the Black Rivers?"

"Now that, I *can* help you with," said Angel, and he spread his wings.

For just a moment, excitement wiped away Jori's fears. After a lifetime of subways and buses, she was about to travel by flying unicorn.

Angel bent his front legs and knelt, allowing Jori to step on his shoulder and swing onto his back. She quickly positioned herself between the strong muscles of his wings.

"Jori."

She looked down at the wolf. Ragar was pacing back and forth, her eyes flashing, her silver coat now a pure, sparkling white.

"Listen to me carefully. Remember that in this world there is no reality, only perception. So nothing here is necessarily what it seems." The wolf's voice grew softer. "But that also means you can make this place what you need it to be. Trust your instincts, girl."

The white fur began to glow, light strobing across it until Jori had to shield her eyes. "Wait, don't go yet!" she shouted. "I don't understand what you mean!"

The glow engulfed the wolf in a single blazing sphere, and her rough voice came from everywhere and nowhere, swirling around Jori like a whirlwind.

"Perhaps you don't now," the voice said. "But you will."

The orb exploded like a starburst.

TEN

PRISONER OF WAR

★

Ragar had vanished. Blinking, Jori lowered her hands. *"Very* nice," she said, a little unsteadily. "Who does her special effects?"

Angel laughed, shaking his head. "Quite a romantic, aren't you? Let's hope my own efforts don't strike you as equally mundane." He lunged forward, almost ripping a hole in the air, and began thundering across the meadow, wings outstretched, head low. Finally, with a powerful thrust of his hind legs, he leaped upward, his glorious wings catching the wind.

Jori gasped and grabbed frantically at Angel's fluttering mane. Soon the valley was a saffron blur beneath them, and they were soaring toward the highest peaks of the Crystal Mountain.

"Impressed yet?" asked Angel.

"Getting there."

The still-bright summit was now just ahead of them, sparkling through delicate wisps of cloud. Angel flew higher, through the flickering lights, and in moments they reached the far side of the mountain.

The rainbows vanished, along with the last remnants of Lisa's dream. Far beneath Angel's hooves, thin tendrils from the Black River wormed through the dreamscape, spitting their poisons into fragile forests, strangling the roots of the dying trees. Jori could see wasted creatures stretched on the ground, gray and utterly still.

She felt herself grow pale.

Angel continued his flight, carrying her further away from the rotting mountain, over a landscape that became increasingly barren. Soon they reached the Black River itself. Jori could hear once more its hungry roar, could see it clawing savagely at either bank. She closed her eyes, refusing to look any more, and counted the beats of Angel's wings.

A rush of cold air slapped her cheeks. Her eyes snapped open, and she looked down to see a place as unlike Avendar as any she could have imagined.

The upper two-thirds of this dreamscape were rugged and barren, sliced by two massive mountain ranges that ran parallel to each other from northeast to southwest. A vast valley separated the two, and a cold, dark lake gleamed in the center. The lower third of the land was cut into sections by three long river valleys, and the areas within seemed equally divided between rolling farmland and stark, rocky moors.

Angel was now flying over the roughest of those sections, under a bank of wet gray clouds. Despite the dim light, Jori could see a dense forest in the distance, and a cluster of tents massed together in a clearing.

Tents like those she had once seen in a movie.

"Angel, wait! Take me down there, to those rocks."

"Why? Your sister is not here."

"No. But someone else I know is."

Angel seemed to pause in mid-flight, hovering as effortlessly as a hummingbird.

"What are you asking me to do, Jori? If you stop here, your sister will wander even further from you. Is this . . . other person really worth that risk?"

Is he? Jori wondered. If he'd just listened to her, back at the old man's, he wouldn't need rescuing at all. And if he was too stupid or spineless to watch out for himself now, why should she worry about him?

Because, another part of her replied, he wouldn't be here in the first place if it weren't for her. She swore to herself.

"Angel, I'm sorry. But I've got to do this."

She could feel the unicorn's frustration as he looked off toward a part of the tapestry she couldn't yet see. But then he nodded.

"All right. I suppose this . . . obstinacy is what will make you a match for Maligor."

Angel shifted position and began to glide toward the ground. As they drew closer, Jori realized that he was growing less distinct, less substantial. In fact, she was actually able to see through him to the rocks beneath. He spoke again, his voice suddenly exhausted and urgent.

"You'll have to jump."

She stared at the rocks.

"From here? Are you *kidding* me?"

"We don't have any choice. I can't enter this place." He was hovering low over the rocky landscape, gasping with the effort. "Now, Jori!"

"I'm going!" She swung a leg over Angel's shoulders and stared at the ground, which was still much too far away to suit her.

"On my count," shouted Angel. "One . . . two . . ."

Jori jumped.

She hit the ground hard and tumbled down a small hill. When she stopped rolling, she struggled to her feet and scanned the sky. Angel was barely visible now, almost indistinguishable from the gray clouds behind him.

"Find your friend, if you must," he called to her. "But then find your sister. Find her, Jori, and bring her home."

He vanished.

Jori felt a shock of loss. Something more than Angel had just vanished, something she couldn't name. But then the frigid wind licked at her face and arms, and she shivered. "Idiot," she muttered, not quite sure if she was referring to Newt or herself. She felt with stiff fingers for the buttons of her jacket, then stopped in surprise. What her hands touched was nothing like a jacket.

She looked down. A gray fur vest was draped over her shoulders, gathered at her waist with a thin leather strip. Plucking the fur away from her chest, she saw some kind of rough woven tunic. It was pulled over a loose shirt of thick, dull-white fabric, and a thinner cotton sheath lay beneath that. Tall boots were strapped around her lower legs, and a fur cap was pulled snugly down on her head. The whole outfit reeked of oil, dirt, and sweat, as though she had been wearing it for weeks.

Something heavy was tied to her back, and she fumbled behind her shoulders. Her fingers brushed against a pack of some kind, and what felt like a wooden handle. She grasped the handle and tugged, bending her knees and leaning forward with the effort. A heavy sword thudded to the ground in front of her.

"Ooooh-kay," she said aloud. "This is different." She stared at the sword, then looked around her. Nothing and no one was visible, but from somewhere far off she could hear faint strains of music, strange and discordant, as though cats were singing.

That must be where the tents are, she thought. And it had better be where Newt is, or I'm in deep trouble.

She replaced the sword and began to stumble across the uneven ground, tripping and swearing and bruising her hands on the sharp rocks. After an hour or so, the woods she had seen from above came into view. The trees grew taller, thicker, more numerous, and soon she found herself in the shadows of a magnificent pine forest, the yowling cats leading her forward.

The trees and bushes formed a natural obstacle course. Small, black-barked shrubs with prickly thorns tore at her clothes, straggling vines hooked the toes of her boots, and the branches of stubborn rowan trees poked at her eyes. Jori found a sharp dagger in a sheath on her belt and began using it to hack through the worst of the maze. But the light was growing dimmer. If she didn't find the camp soon . . .

A branch snapped off to one side, and she squinted in that direction. A short distance away, a tall figure disappeared into a copse of trees. She began to yell, but then realized that this wasn't her dream, and that she was a girl, alone.

She moved as quickly as she could in the direction the figure had gone, shoving her way through a cat's cradle of vines. She heard laughter from just ahead and dropped to a crouch. Moving one leafy branch to the side, she could just make out the figure she'd seen before—tall and thin, not stocky enough to be a grown man. Then a second figure came out of the woods. This one was equally tall, but stronger, more muscular. He held up a large grouse in his right hand.

"What do ye think?"

The thinner boy put a hand to his chin and seemed to consider. "Well, I think it'll feed you and me. But what about the others?"

"Ach, we just won't tell 'em."

The thin boy laughed. "Good plan, Kieran, but William sent us out for boar. We'd best try a little longer. I just came from there—" he pointed in Jori's direction—"so let's head toward th' stream." But Jori was staring at his face. He had thin features, yes, and a nose too big for his face. And long, sandy hair that fell over his eyes.

"Newt?"

She had only whispered the name, but the thin boy's face froze, as though he had heard her. He turned away, moving next to the other youth, and Jori saw him bend his head to the other's ear. His companion nodded, and they suddenly moved off in two different directions.

"Damn." Jori scrambled after the boy who looked like Newt. But he was moving too swiftly for her, and within minutes she had lost him entirely. Worse, she could no longer hear the sounds of the camp. She stopped, frustrated.

Then felt something sharp in the small of her back.

"And what d'we have here?" said a quiet voice. "A spy?"

Jori raised her hands slowly, her heart thudding.

"I wouldn't reach for my sword, if I were you. Not if ye ever want to reach for anything again."

Jori started to answer, then remembered her other fear.

"I'm not a spy," she said gruffly, trying to sound as male as possible.

"Of course ye aren't. That's why yer sneakin' after us."

Jori's temper started to flicker. "I'm not sneaking. And I told you, I'm not a spy." There was no answer. "Can I at least see who I'm talking to? And could you maybe get that sword out of my back?"

"I could," said the same quiet voice. "But turn around slow."

Keeping her arms raised, Jori turned to confront her captor. She squinted through the shadows and could just make out the tall, lanky figure she had first seen. And now there was no question who it was.

"Newt!" She leaped toward him, but he took a quick step backward and thrust his sword toward her.

"Back off, laddie," the boy said. "And watch what ye call me." He yelled over his shoulder, keeping his eyes fixed on her. "Kieran! Over here!"

Jori stared at him, confused. Then she heard the crackle of branches breaking underfoot. A moment later, the second youth stepped into the clearing, his own sword raised. He quickly took in the scene in front of him.

"Good work, Nathaniel!" he said, slapping the first boy's shoulder. "Ye caught much better game then I did."

Nathaniel. Then it *was* Newt.

"Newt, you idiot, just look! It's me, Jori!" She yanked the cap off her head and stepped into a weak patch of light that had struggled through the branches. "See?" she said, pointing to her short red hair and turning the scarred side of her face toward him. "Jori!"

The older youth, Kieran, looked from her to his companion. "What's this, Nathaniel? D'ye know this lad?"

"I've never seen him before in my life."

Jori stamped her foot in frustration. "Oh, for godssakes. I'm not a 'lad'! I'm a girl." She glared at Newt. "I'm *Jori!*"

But there was no recognition in his eyes.

Kieran circled her, looking her up and down. "So ye're a girl, are ye? Not our usual sort o' spy, I must admit. What do ye think, Nathaniel?"

"I think we're not stupid. That we don't take any chances."

Kieran nodded. "All right. Agreed. But I'm not certain it's a good idea to bring a lass into the camp." He picked up Jori's cap and shoved it back down over her hair.

"Keep it on," he said. "And perhaps ye should go back to usin' that low voice I heard before. It was really verra convincin'." Jori wanted to kick him. But then he winked, and one corner of his mouth twitched upward.

"All right, then," Kieran continued. "Let's head into camp, see what William has to say."

Newt nodded grimly and motioned for Jori to turn around. He yanked her hands behind her and bound them tightly with a thin leather strip. A frightening thought thrust itself into her brain. What if Newt really *had* forgotten her?

That could be part of the tapestry's power—to steal memories. If so, then she really was a prisoner here.

The three of them walked in silence. Kieran sometimes pulled alongside to give her a reassuring smile, but Newt himself seemed agitated, nervous, constantly glancing backward as though he'd heard something. Once, following his gaze, Jori thought she saw a flash of silver in the darkness. She felt a rush of hope. Could the wolf have followed her here? But if something was shadowing them, it remained hidden.

Soon, Jori once more became aware of the howling cats. The sound grew louder, splitting into a dozen voices accompanied by harsh wheezing chords. Within no more than fifteen minutes, the two boys had brought her to the edge of a clearing. They paused for a moment while Newt checked her bindings, and she was able to survey the scene.

The camp was a riot of noise and activity. Jokes and insults were being hurled like rocks, and coarse laughter mixed with the words of a raucous drinking song. The singers were accompanied by a man who was forcing a tortured yowl out of a thin pipe and small bellows. The singing cats, thought Jori, wincing.

A dozen more men crouched around a smoky pit, chewing on strips of venison cut from a dripping carcass that hung over the fire. Others lounged around the camp, cleaning their weapons or gambling. Several of these men were older, with gray, craggy faces, and Jori could imagine any one of them stretched out comfortably in a chair with a half-dozen grandchildren clamoring for stories. Others were young, a few still beardless.

Despite the camaraderie, tension laced the air, and many of the men sat silently, staring at the ground. Jori noticed a smaller group huddled outside one of the tents, bending intently over marks one of them was scratching in the earth with a stick.

She looked around warily as she was led into the clearing. All conversation stopped, and the yowling of the cats died away.

"What's this, now?" Jori looked toward the voice and saw a tall, powerful man rising from the group near the tent. He strode toward them, his long hair flowing like a lion's mane. Every other man in the camp turned to watch him. Of course, Jori thought. Kieran said William. William Wallace.

He stopped in front of them, looking at Jori skeptically. "And is this all ye caught on your huntin' trip, lads? He won't make much of a meal."

Kieran and Newt looked at each other, grinning.

"No, sir," said Newt. "He won't. But he was off by himself, not far from the camp. I thought he might be an English scout."

The older man looked at Jori, who stared at him defiantly. His eyes narrowed, and for a moment she was certain he was seeing her for what she really was. But then he nodded.

"Good work, Nathaniel."

Newt grinned, his cheeks flushed with pride. But when his eyes flicked back to Jori, the smile vanished.

"All right," said Wallace. "We'll see what he knows. But I have more important things t'deal with right now. Tie th' boy up in one of the tents. We'll deal with him later."

"Nathaniel," said Kieran. "Can ye can handle it?"

"Aye. I can." He walked up to Jori and shoved her toward one of the tents. "Move. Over there."

Jori pictured herself turning and kneeing him in a strategic location. But she forced herself to remain silent and let him take her to one of the tents that ringed the campsite. As they moved through the groups of men, they slapped him on the back, grunting their approval.

"Newt, would you just—"

"Be quiet," he said, finally shoving her through the flaps of the tent. He jerked his head toward a crumpled blanket in one corner. She plopped down in despair, and Newt bound her ankles with another thin strip of leather. Then he stood, gave her one last, angry look, and strode out of the tent.

Jori struggled briefly with the bindings, then slumped, defeated. This was great. Trapped here for who knew how long, while time continued to twist and flow all through the tapestry. She wracked her brain, trying desperately to figure out what to do next. And then she heard a rough voice speaking quietly outside the tent—or maybe just in the back of her mind.

In this world, there is no reality, only perception. Make this place what you need it to be.

"I hear you, wolf," she whispered. She thought quickly.

"Hey, out there! I demand to talk to someone. Anyone! Now!" She raised her voice, getting louder, more annoying—seeking a level of obnoxiousness that would force Newt to come in and shut her up.

The flaps of the tent parted.

"Well?" asked Kieran.

She looked up in surprise. She needed Newt, not his fabrication. But then she saw a water flask hanging from Kieran's belt, and improvised.

"Well, first of all, I could use some water. Or were you planning to let me die of thirst?"

Kieran blinked. But then he crouched next to her and put his flask to her lips.

"Drink," he said. As she gulped down the water, his eyes darted to her tightly bound wrists and ankles. "It looks like my brother may have overdone things a wee bit."

Jori pulled her lips from the flask. "Brother?"

"Unfortunately." But he said this with a grin. "Well, there's no need to cut off the blood. I'll loosen the bindings a bit."

"Why don't you just take them off altogether?"

One eyebrow went up. "Because I'm not that daft. Why would I free someone we found spyin' on us from the woods?"

"Come on, Kieran. You know I'm not here to spy on you."

"I do, do I?"

"Yes. The truth is, I've never even been away from home before."

"Ah. And where is home, if ye' don't mind me askin'? What does yer family do?"

Jori's brain stuttered. But she searched her memory for another scene from the old DVD she had watched many months before.

"We raise sheep."

Kieran nodded slowly. "Ye're from th' Uplands, then."

Jori had no idea where or what the Uplands were, so she hoped his comment wasn't some kind of trick. "Yes. The Uplands." He nodded, and she relaxed. "But my family's in trouble, Kieran."

Kieran looked at her skeptically. "Oh really. What kind of trouble?"

Jori worked a tremble into her lips, pinched her wrist to force tears to her eyes. "Some men . . . they came one night and burned our cottage." Jori allowed the tears to stream down her face.

Kieran's face softened, his eyes flicking to Jori's arm and the right side of her face. For once, the scars were working in her favor.

"Now my father's dead, and my sister . . . She's gone. Kidnapped."

She saw Kieren's jaw tighten. "D'ye have any idea who it was took her?"

Jori shook her head—then remembered what Newt had said to William Wallace. "We did hear English voices."

Kieran's eyes blazed, and he slammed his fist onto his thigh. "Edward's mongrels, rot their souls! Thinkin' they own everything that's Scottish—even the people." He stood, his jaw clenched. "Wait here." He stormed from the tent, striking the flap so hard that it tore.

Jori smiled, pleased with herself. A few minutes later, Kieran reappeared, and she pulled the look of despair back onto her face. He strode over to her, pulled out a knife, and slashed the strips that bound her wrists and ankles.

"All right—Jori, was it? Come wi' me."

She followed Kieran out of the tent. Most of the men were already asleep, snoring loudly beneath heavy furs. But on a log near the fire, staring into the flames, sat William Wallace. As they approached, he turned his head, smiled gently, and reached for Jori's hand. His fingers were strong and warm, his eyes so intense that everything suddenly took on an immediate, overpowering reality.

"I'm sorry for your troubles, lass."

"Thank you, sir," she whispered.

Wallace's face was edged with a deep pain of his own. Jori remembered the more tragic parts of his legend—the deaths of his father and brother, and the murder of his young wife by an English soldier. She wrapped that knowledge into her plan.

"I'm afraid, sir. I'm so afraid of what might have happened to my sister."

Wallace said nothing, his eyes no longer seeing her.

"It will kill my mother if I don't find her. Even knowing the worst would be better than not knowing at all." The truth of what she was saying suddenly struck her, and her throat tightened. "Can you help me?" she whispered. "Please?"

He focused on her once more.

"Aye. I can." He looked over at Kieran. "All right, lad. Listen to me. As ye know, I canna leave the camp. But it's critical that we know more about our enemy—where they're positioned, how many there are. Do ye' understand?"

Kieran nodded. "Yes, sir."

"Good. I want ye to be my scout. Head toward the river, travelin' by night when ye' can. See what ye can find out."

Newt suddenly darted into the firelight. "What about me, sir? Two sets of eyes are better than one."

Wallace laughed. "I thought I'd be hearin' from ye, lad. There's nothin' your brother does that you don't want t'do, too."

Click, Jori thought smugly. Part two of her plan had fallen neatly into place.

"All right," said Wallace. "Go with him, then." He glanced at Jori. "And I want you to take the girl with you."

Newt's expression froze, and Jori bit back a grin.

"Are you certain, sir?" Newt asked. "She'll just slow us down."

"But while you're looking for the English, it may be that you'll find her sister as well. And if anything's happened to her . . . ," his face darkened, "then come back and tell me. She *will* be avenged."

The next afternoon, Jori watched Kieran gather the provisions they would need, rolling them into tight bundles they could carry on their backs. Newt helped him—filling their water flasks, honing their weapons—but he never said a word to Jori. When they were nearly ready, William Wallace came over to the boys with a piece of tanned hide, on which was a crudely drawn map.

"This is where we are," he said. "Only two day's walk west o' the Tweed." He pointed to a wavy line that began halfway down the map and curved to the southeast. "Since the girl's home is in the Uplands, it's likely that th' English who attacked her family first traveled upriver, then crossed over. With any luck, they'll still be camped along the banks."

As Jori listened, she began struggling to lift her heavy pack. She heard someone walk up next to her.

"Ye've had a long, hard time of it," Kieran said. "Why don't ye let me carry some o' yer things?" She looked at him indignantly, and he stepped back, raising one hand.

"On th' other hand," he said slowly, "maybe you should carry some o' mine." He grinned, and Jori started to smile back. Then she caught herself. Don't be an idiot, she thought. He's another figment.

Finally, it was time to leave. Just before they set out, William Wallace walked over to Jori and motioned her toward him. He put a gentle hand on her cheek. "I'll be prayin' for ye, lass," he said quietly. "I'll be prayin' that you and your sister will be travelin' home together soon."

This time, Jori's tears were real.

ELEVEN
ALONG THE RIVER

The beginning of their journey was uneventful, but painfully quiet. Newt kept his distance from Jori and still showed no signs of recognizing her. So now what, she thought. Will I be stuck on some never-ending nature hike?

She noticed Kieran watching her, and swallowed nervously. Please, don't let him ask me about anything else, she thought. One more question about the Uplands or sheep shearing, and her little invention would fall apart.

But he seemed more curious than suspicious, and was casting worried looks at Newt, as well. Finally, he moved next to Jori and leaned toward her like a conspirator.

"If we're to be travelin' together, Jori, I think it's important that you ye know a little more about us. T'build a bit of trust, y'understand. For example, did I ever tell ye about the time this brother o' mine decided he wanted to try his hand at fishin'?"

She looked up, confused, but he tilted his head toward Newt and winked. She noticed again the crooked smile, the laughter in his eyes. She winked back.

"No, Kieran, I don't think you ever did."

"Good. Then I'll tell ye now. It's actually quite an amusin' tale.

"Now, ye'd never guess it, but not all that long ago, Nathaniel was a scrawny lad, with no muscle to him at all. In fact, his only chore was to feed the chickens—and he wasn't even very good at that, since the chickens kept knockin' him down."

Jori saw Newt turn his head slightly to listen.

"So he comes to me one day, and he says, 'Kieran, I need to be doin' more to help around here. Now, I know I'm too puny to manage a bow, and I can't lift a scythe when it's time to work the fields. But even a skinny lad like me can hold a pole over a stretch o' water and catch some fish. So will ye' teach me, brother?' he says."

A grumble came from up ahead.

"I never asked you to teach me how to fish."

"Ach, now don't be embarrassed, Nathaniel. Besides, who's tellin' this story, me or you?"

"You."

"Then stop talkin'." Kieran focused again on Jori. "So we take two poles and head into the Highlands, toward one of them lochs that sits on the great canal between the mountains. I show Nathaniel how to string his pole and tie his hook and set the bait. It's takin' him forever, but when I try to help he says, 'Leave me alone, can't ye?' So I do—I leave him alone. Finally, his hook's in th' water. And it's not verra long before he has a bite."

"And . . . ?" asked Jori.

"Well, he plants his feet and starts yankin' on the pole. But whatever he's got on the other end is pullin' back just as hard. 'Help me, Kieran!' he yells, sweat pourin' from him. 'But Nathaniel,' I say, 'ye told me that ye wanted to do it yerself.' And I fold my arms, and I watch.

"Then—whoosh! A monstrous big head comes shootin' out of the water, sittin' on top of a long, thin neck. The thing's as tall as a tree and ugly as a toad, but Nathaniel still won't let go of the pole. Soon he's swingin' out over the lake, hangin' on like a dog with a bone, and I'm not sure anymore who's caught who.

"'I've got it, Kieran!' he yells down ta me. 'Get the net!'

"'I'm guessin' the net might be a wee bit small,' I shout. 'Ye might want to think aboot throwin' this one back!'

"'Never!' cries Nathaniel. And he pulls himself hand over hand up the pole until he can wrap his legs around it, too."

Jori sputtered as she pictured Newt dangling like a forgotten appetizer from the sea serpent's mouth. And Newt himself was finally smiling.

"So what happened?" asked Jori.

"Well, it seemed that although Nathaniel was wagin' a terrible battle against the monster, the monster didn't even know he was there. It just kept munchin' on the fishing line like it was a piece of grass. Finally, the beast chews down to the pole itself, and his first bite snaps it into two pieces. Nathaniel drops straight into the lake.

"Well, he pops back up, sputterin' and swearin', and starts swimmin' after the creature. 'C'mon, Kieran!' he yells. 'I can still catch it! Throw me a rope!' But jus' then, the beast belches, turns, and starts glidin' away. Its neck disappears, and then the head. A moment later, and there's nothin' left of him but ripples." Kieran sighed. "Poor Nathaniel never did catch a fish."

Both Jori and Newt were choking on laughter. "And where did you say all this happened?" asked Jori, gasping.

"At the big loch in the Highlands. Loch Ness."

They burst out laughing again.

From that moment, Newt no longer walked apart from them. In fact, he and Kieran both entertained Jori with stories about their life in the village and their adventures with

William Wallace. Newt even smiled at her occasionally, or helped her adjust her pack when it started to slip.

By the time dusk had fallen, they had reached the River Tweed. Every muscle in Jori's body was aching, and she winced with each step. Eventually Kieran noticed.

"Why don't ye rest a bit," he said. "I'll go on ahead an' look for a place where we can make camp for the night. Nathaniel, stay with her." He nodded toward a fallen log, then set off along the riverbank.

Jori dropped onto the log, rubbing her thighs and shins. Her feet felt swollen, and her shoulders sagged with fatigue. How am I ever going to get up again? she thought. She heard Newt walk up next to her. His voice came in a whisper.

"I'm sorry, Jori."

Her head snapped up. "Newt?" He nodded, and she jumped up, the pain forgotten, not sure if she wanted to hug him or punch him. "God, Newt. You had me scared to death! I thought you didn't remember me!"

"I *didn't* remember you. Not at first."

"So when . . . ?"

Newt smiled wryly. "I think when you started yelling at me."

"So why'd you tie me up? Why didn't you say something then, before we got to the camp?"

"I wasn't ready yet."

"What? To admit you knew me?"

"Yeah. No. It's just . . . it's been so different for me here. No one thinks I'm . . . no one thinks I can't handle myself. I'm just one of William's band."

In her mind, Jori saw once more the welcome Newt had received on his return to camp, the pride each man seemed to have in him.

Newt went on. "And you see how it is with Kieran and me."

"I do see, Newt. He's a great brother." Jori spoke the next words gently, deliberately. "It's a wonderful dream."

His smile faded. "What are you talking about?"

"Newt, don't. If you know who I am, then you know *exactly* what I'm talking about. The tapestry."

But Newt had stopped listening. He stared down the path in front of them. "Kieran should've been back by now. I'd better go see where he is."

"Listen to me. I know what all this means to you. But none of it's real. Only you are, and I am. And Lisa, if we can find her."

He jerked toward her, his face anguished. "It's real! Don't say it's not real! Because if it isn't . . ."

"Newt—"

A branch snapped, and Jori looked to that side, expecting to see Kieran. Instead, two dark figures detached themselves from the shadows.

"Well, well. Look at wot's got lost in the woods."

Two men slouched in front of her, dressed in the tattered remnants of uniforms. The first was a giant, thick-bodied and slow, who looked pieced together from parts of a butchered ox. The second man was smaller, quicker, his nose and cheekbones sharp planes on his narrow face. Jori could see a still-raw scar on his neck, stretching across his windpipe.

"Looks like nice full packs you 'ave there," he said, his voice rasping like sandpaper. "An' me friend and me is in need of some victuals. So why don't you just 'and it all over, like good lads."

Jori waited for Newt to do something, say something. To play out one of the scenes he'd watched so many times, alone in his apartment at night. But he didn't move. She looked toward him and found he was staring not at the two men—but at her.

"Newt," she said. "What is it?"

He didn't answer.

"So wot's it gonna be, boys?"

Jori forced her eyes back to the two men and slipped her dagger from its sheath, her palms cold with sweat. "Get away from us," she said, lowering her voice.

The man clicked his tongue. "Not very friendly, are ya' boy?"

He feinted toward the right, and Jori swung the dagger to follow him. At the same moment, the big man jumped toward Newt and slammed him into a tree, smashing his head against the trunk. Jori cried out and spun in his direction. A moment later she felt her wrist being crushed in a vise-like grip, and her dagger dropped to the ground. The thin man snatched it up, yanking her towards him. Her neck snapped backwards and the cap flew off her head.

The man laughed, an ugly, toneless sound.

"Well, well," he said, eyes narrowing. "Not a boy at all, are ya? Those scars of yers had me fooled." He looked her up and down, then grinned, revealing black, broken teeth. For the first time, Jori felt fear. What was going on? Why wasn't Newt acting out the heroics he'd set the stage for? She looked toward the woods, searching desperately for Kieran . . . or for the flash of silver she'd seen the day before. But then the thin man twisted her around, threw one arm across her neck, and began whispering foul things in her ear. His huge companion, watching from where he held Newt pinned, grinned stupidly.

The hell with this, Jori thought. She cried out, jabbing one elbow into the thin man's ribs and kicking backwards at his knees with all her strength.

She heard a snap, and the man yelped with pain, his grip loosening. Jori wriggled from his grasp and scrambled several yards away, fumbling for a thick branch that lay just in front of her. She stood upright, the branch held to her shoulder like a baseball bat, and turned back toward the thin man. Fury pumped through her veins, pounded in her head, almost deafened her.

"Come on," she spat at him, her fingers digging into the wood. "Just try."

His face twisted. "I'll do a lot more than try."

A furious roar tore the air, and Jori was blinded by a streak of white-hot light. A moment later she heard a strangled cry and a ripping sound, and the thin man screamed in agony. The light dimmed, and Jori saw a wild, raging figure whirl away from him, teeth red with blood.

"Ragar!"

The wolf looked at her, eyes blazing, jaws parted in a murderous grin.

"I'm okay," Jori yelled. "Get the other one." She lunged forward, whipping her branch at the thin man. He dodged the blow, throwing her off balance, then limped forward again, dagger raised.

Jori straightened and swung again, the branch connecting with a dull crack. The man stumbled backwards, his hand flying to his skull. Nearby, Jori saw the wolf dragging the giant to the ground, her teeth buried in a bloody mass of torn skin and muscle. Newt remained slumped against the tree, watching.

"Newt!" she screamed. "What are you waiting for?"

He turned his head and stared at her. And suddenly she knew.

Newt didn't want to help her.

Jori felt a fury far worse than anything she had felt for the two deserters. At that same moment, she saw Ragar turn slowly from the giant to glare at Newt instead. She stalked toward him, teeth bared, until he cowered against the trunk. She growled, revealing her fangs, and Jori heard her speak.

"What are you really afraid of, boy? And what are you trying to prove?"

Her voice went lower, and Jori could no longer hear what the wolf was saying. But the condemnation was unmistakable, and Newt turned his head, his face crimson. Finally he nodded, pulled himself upright, and looked toward the woods.

A moment later there was the sound of someone running through the brush, a hoarse cry, a voice yelling out their names. Kieran burst into clearing, taking in the scene with one glance. His eyes widened when he saw the wolf almost at Newt's throat, and he raised his sword.

Newt shook his head. "No," he said, looking again at Ragar, then Jori. "She's not going to hurt me."

Ragar's furious posture relaxed. She nodded at Newt, then leaped to one side and disappeared into the forest.

Newt stared after her for a moment, then turned toward the big man, who had struggled back to his feet. As Jori watched in astonishment, Newt yelled like a madman and lunged at the giant, his sword held high over one shoulder. The giant lurched backwards, fumbling for a short ax that hung from his belt. Just as he reached it, Newt slashed at the man's upper arm. There was an agonized bellow, and the ax dropped to the ground.

The big man's eyes were mad with pain. He leaned forward, scooping up a huge rock in his ham-sized hand, and roared blindly toward Newt, ready to crush his skull.

But Newt stood firm, raising his sword at the last moment. The giant ran into his blade.

The man's pig eyes bulged, and his arm dropped to his side. Newt held the sword steady, driving it deep into the giant's body. Blood bubbled out around the edges of the blade. A moment later the giant crumpled to his knees and fell to one side, dead. Newt stood over him, eyes blazing.

Jori turned away, shaken, and saw Kieran standing with his own sword pointed at the heart of the thin man, who lay on his back on the ground.

"Get up," Kieran said. "Unless ye'd prefer never to get up again."

The thin man groaned to his feet, his scalp one long, ugly gash.

"Good," said Kieran. "Ye can walk." He motioned with his sword. "Now go. Get out o' here."

The man stared at the body of the giant, then stumbled into the trees. Kieran turned to Jori, his eyes sick with worry.

"Are ye all right, Jori? They didn't harm ye?"

"I'm fine."

He released a long breath, then touched her face gently. "Thank God."

The touch startled her. But Kieran had already turned away and was looking at Newt.

"We shouldn't even try goin' further today," he said. "I found a clearing not far from here. We can stop there and camp for the night."

Newt nodded, not speaking.

"I'll just make sure our friend is gone, first," Kieran said. He headed in the direction the thin man had disappeared.

Which left Jori standing with Newt.

"You almost got me killed," she said.

"What are you talking about?"

"Those two goons only showed up when we started talking about the tapestry. You wanted to get rid of me."

Newt didn't reply.

"You really think I'm such a big threat? That you can't survive away from this place?"

"Shut up," he said, jaw tight with fury. "Why are you even here? Everything was fine until you showed up. You and that damn wolf." He stalked away into the shadows.

Jori watched him leave, astonished. Then she kicked at a fallen log, swearing at Newt, swearing at herself. Why *was* she here? She should have stayed with Angel, should have gone straight after Lisa.

"And you would never have forgiven yourself."

A short distance away, the trees shimmered. Ragar reappeared, a ghost in the darkness.

"But what's the use?" Jori asked. "He doesn't want to leave."

"He must. The longer he holds onto this world, the harder it will be for him to relinquish."

"So what do I do?" She remembered her earlier scheme, back at the camp. "Maybe if I talk to Kieran."

"He is a part of this. Be wary of him, girl."

"Of Kieran? But—" Ragar growled, and Jori was startled to see the wolf staring right past her, it's hackles raised and bristling. Jori's stomach heaved. Had the scavenger returned? She turned around slowly. To her relief, she saw only Kieran, already returned from his brief reconnaissance.

"Well, I don't think our friend is plannin' to come back." He stopped, his expression darkening. Jori glanced back toward the wolf, but she had vanished.

"Where's Nathaniel?" Kieran asked, looking around angrily. "Did he just *leave* ye? After everything that happened?"

"No!" Jori thought quickly. "He just had to . . . Well, you know. He said he'd catch up with us."

Kieran's expression relaxed, and he smiled. "Ah. Well, that's good t'hear. That is, if talkin' about someone movin' his bowels is ever good t'hear." He smiled at her. "Come wi' me, then. We'll start th' fire ourselves."

They walked side by side along the riverbank, gathering tinder and kindling as they went. They said little, but Jori felt comfortable in the silence. Safe, as well. Soon, they reached the clearing. Kieran brushed the fallen leaves and weeds from a wide area, then crouched and began arranging bits of twig and moss. Taking out a piece of flint, he struck a spark in the moss and blew steadily, trying to coax the tiny flicker into a flame.

"Ach," he muttered. "I knew I should have packed a campfire."

Jori smiled. Strange. In many ways, he looked and acted like Newt, down to his odd sense of humor and rambling stories. But he had all the strength and confidence that Newt lacked. Was that his role in this world?

"Nathaniel is certainly taking his time," said Kieran, interrupting her thoughts. "I hope he wasn't wounded in a sensitive area."

Jori laughed, and Kieran grinned. Soon a good fire blazed in front of them, and they sat before it, close together, gazing contentedly into the crackling flames. Jori glanced at Kieran and caught him watching her, his face intent, his hair red-gold in the firelight. His eyes dropped, and he suddenly seemed very interested in a twig he was bending in his hands.

"Jori," he said finally. "I was wonderin'. Do ye . . . like my brother?"

She wasn't quite sure how to respond. "He's all right, I guess."

"Ah," said Kieran, still focusing on the twig. "Because I saw him lookin' at ye before, kind o' strange. And so I wondered if you—"

Jori almost laughed. "No. Nothing like that. Besides, if he's 'lookin' at me strange,' it's probably because I *am* strange."

"Well, that's true."

"Thanks a lot."

Kieran finally raised his eyes. "No, I don't mean—It's just that ye'll go off on your own to find yer sister, stand up t' two grown men with nothin' but a branch in your hands . . ." His lopsided smile returned. "Ye're not like any girl I've ever met."

"I get that a lot."

"It's a good thing, Jori." He leaned forward, his eyes holding hers. And then, hesitantly, he kissed her.

Shock spun through her, then a bolt of pure happiness. And then a strange, beautiful pain, as the kiss seared away her scars—scars she only now realized had formed within her. To her surprise, she began to cry, clinging tightly to Kieran. He held her tenderly, murmuring words she had so desperately needed to hear.

A loud crash made them both jump.

"What's going on?"

Newt was staring at them, stunned, a pile of logs at his feet.

"Nothing!" Jori said, wiping at her eyes. "Nothing's going on."

"Not now, anyhow," said Kieran. And Jori found herself wishing violently that Newt would just disappear.

But Newt stayed where he was, fists clenched.

"So maybe the two of you would like to be alone? Maybe I should just head back to camp?"

"Don't be daft, Nathaniel," laughed Kieran. He squeezed Jori's hand, then stood and walked over to his brother. "Nothin' happened. Besides, we still have work to do for William."

Newt's eyes narrowed. "I don't know about that. Do we, Jori? Do we have work to do?"

Jori looked from Newt to Kieran and back again, and for a moment their images swam together. "Yes. We do. It's just that things are a little different now. But New—Nathaniel, that doesn't mean Kieran can't still help us."

"Oh, and you'd like that, wouldn't you?"

Jori's head cleared, and she blew out her breath in exasperation. "Oh, shut up. He's *your*—" she caught herself, "brother!"

Kieran's eyebrows shot up. "Did I miss somethin' here?"

"No," said Newt, still glaring at Jori. "You didn't miss anything. Just a little conversation Jori and I had earlier."

"Listen, Kieran," said Jori, looking for a thread of logic that could lead them out of this strange tangle of events. "I'm worried about my sister. I know you two have to follow your orders, but I need to move faster." She looked pointedly at Newt. "With you or without you."

Jori watched Newt's face shift through a dozen different expressions. Finally, he shot her a murderous look, then turned toward Kieran.

"You can keep scouting, Kieran. I'll go ahead with Jori and try to help her find her sister. And then . . . I'll come back."

Kieran nodded. "Aye, Nathaniel. 'Tis certainly the right thing to do." Newt folded his arms and stared defiantly at Jori, who felt a sudden, small ache of loss. Then Kieran spoke again.

"Just before we left, though, William told me that as the eldest, I'm to make sure that neither of ye come to any harm." He winked at Jori. "So I suppose I'll have to come along, as well."

Jori turned to hide the grin that threatened to split her face. Newt, though, seemed confused. "But I don't need . . . I mean, I thought . . ."

Kieran ignored him. "So tell me, Jori. Where is it we're goin'?"

Jori took a deep, relieved breath. "Let's just keep following the river. I have a feeling it will take us where we need to go."

TWELVE

THE CROSSING

The next morning, the three headed once more down river, in the direction of the North Sea. Newt walked a little ahead, shoulders hunched, and silent as a mule. Jori finally moved up alongside him.

"You okay?"

"What do you care?"

"Look, I'm sorry I blew up yesterday. I know you wouldn't have let things go too far. You just wanted to keep me from—"

"Shut up." He glared at her. "Just shut up, okay? I don't need any of your psychoanalysis."

Jori's temper flared, and she dropped back to walk next to Kieran. He smiled, nodded toward Newt. "Don't worry. He'll get over it."

"Who's worried?" She started an animated conversation with Kieran, laughing at his jokes, complimenting him on the battle the day before. With every sentence, Newt's shoulders drooped lower.

Good, she thought.

Soon, though, she found herself listening to Kieran less and less, aware that the land they traveled through was shifting again. The endless hills and rocky soil had become a dull, flat plain that could have existed almost anywhere.

The river, too, was changing, its lively waters now dark and smelling faintly of sulfur. And no matter how long they traveled, there was no indication that they were any closer to the sea. No scent of salt water, no hint of a fresh breeze.

"None o' this looks familiar," said Kieran, frowning. "And yet we couldn't be off our path."

Jori didn't reply.

By the time they had traveled another two hours, iron gray clouds choked the sky, lightning flashing in their bellies. The river itself grew violent, smashing against jagged rocks that pierced the surface. From the north, a second river roared down toward the first, the two crashing together to form one howling black serpent.

Jori glanced at Newt. He was staring at the churning waters, his face pale. *He knows it's the end of his dreamscape,* she thought, and felt a twinge of pity. Then a harsh light distracted her. She looked across the south-flowing river to the land beyond it. There, where the dark clouds began to thin, a brutal sun beat down on an endless expanse of blood-red rock and sand.

She could see something else, as well—an odd light on the horizon, glowing beyond the dark silhouette of a dune. Squinting, she could just make out ivory towers atop a bank of massive white walls. *No,* she thought, wishing she hadn't looked. *It's enough I stopped for Newt. No one would expect me to chase after anyone else, especially those two.*

"What're you looking at?" Kieran asked, walking up next to her. She pointed across the river.

Confusion clouded his face. "I've never seen anythin' like that before. Ever."

"I know." Jori stared a while longer, trying to convince herself that what lay on the other side was no concern of hers. But then she heard Ragar's voice from the night before: *. . . and you would never have forgiven yourself.* She shook her head and gave up the struggle. Even Marisa and Derek didn't deserve to rot inside a spider's web.

"We need to go there, Kieran. Beyond that hill."

Kieran looked at her curiously. "And why would ye think this?"

"I just do. You'll have to trust me."

He smiled, reaching over to touch the side of her face. He never even seems to notice the scars, she thought, wonderingly. "I do trust ye, Jori. And more."

The pleasure-pain rushed through her again. Self-conscious, she glanced toward Newt. He was watching them, his expression unreadable.

"Kieran, let me talk to Nathaniel for a minute, all right?"

He glanced over at the other boy. "Ye're braver than I am. But go ahead." Jori walked toward Newt, who looked away as she approached.

"Come on, Newt, quit it. I need to talk to you."

"No one's stopping you."

"But I need you to listen, too. It's about Derek and Marisa. They're over there, across the river."

For a moment, Newt didn't respond. "How do you know that?"

"Because I saw them in the tapestry room, at the old man's."

"So you saw them. That doesn't mean they're across the river. They could be anywhere."

"No. The red rock, those towers—they were woven into the tapestry, Newt."

He remained silent. But his expression told her that he knew.

Kieran rejoined them, looking from one of them to the other, his brow furrowed. "Are ye all right, Nathaniel?" he asked, touching his shoulder.

Newt shook off his hand. "I don't know." He walked to the river's edge, stood silently for several minutes.

"Well," he said, finally, "are we going to cross this thing, or not?"

Jori and Kieran joined him, staring at the churning black water. The river wasn't that wide—no more than twenty yards or so across—but it was cold as a glacier, with a current that looked powerful enough to pound a tree into kindling. There were no bridges anywhere, not even a fallen log.

"So what should we do?" she asked Kieran. "How can we cross it?"

"Well, we can head downstream a bit, see if there's a shallower place to cross. But we canna be certain there is."

"Maybe I have an idea," said Newt. Jori looked around in surprise. Newt was peering further downriver, to where a large dead tree on the opposite bank had been partially uprooted and leaned low over the water. "Kieran. Give me your rope."

Jori raised her eyebrows at Newt's brusque command. But Kieran just nodded and pulled a long coil from his pack. Newt took it and moved just a few yards upstream from the dead tree, to where a spidery knot of wood lay on the ground.

Freeing one end of the rope, Newt bent down and wound it around the wood, knotting it several times in the process. Then he stood upright and let out several more feet. Gripping it tightly in his right hand, he raised the wooden weight and started swinging it in a circle over his head.

"Ah," said Kieran. "I have a very clever brother."

"What do you mean?"

"If he can get th' rope anchored in that tree, we can all use it to pull ourselves across." Kieran seemed both proud and somewhat jealous. "I don't know if I'd've thought o' that."

Newt kept swinging the rope, letting it out bit by bit, and soon the wooden anchor spun at least fifteen feet from his head. He released it with a grunt, and the rope sailed through the air, arcing over the water and toward the tree on the other side. Jori held her breath. But the rope splashed into the river more than ten feet short of its goal.

The current immediately seized the wood and whipped it downstream. Determinedly, Newt yanked it back to shore. The rope was now black with mud and weeds from the riverbed, but he clawed off the worst of it and ignored the added weight. Gripping the line in his hand, he once more began to swing it overhead. A minute later, it flew from his grasp, but this time the branch fell even shorter than before.

"'Tis a bloody brilliant idea, Nathaniel," said Kieran. "But why don't ye let me do the throwin'? My arms have a little more muscle on 'em than yours."

"No," said Newt. "I'll do it." He yanked on the rope again, dragging it from the muck of the river, and once more started to swing it. He threw again—with the same result. Doggedly, he repeated the process two more times. But with each attempt the wooden weight dropped farther from the tree, and his hands grew red with blood.

"Listen, New—thaniel," said Jori. "You're hurting yourself, and the rocks are tearing up the rope. Let Kieran try."

Exhausted and frustrated, Newt threw down the heavy rope. "Sure. Go ahead, Kieran. Give her a thrill."

Jori started toward him, but Newt waved her away. Kieran picked up the rope from the ground. As Newt had done, he whirled the heavy wood block in a wide arc over his head. But the circle was larger this time, the speed much greater. He eyed the dead tree carefully, counted under his breath, and released the rope.

The chunk of wood flew directly into the branches and fell neatly between two thick limbs. Kieran gripped the rope, pulled it hand over hand until it was taut, and then yanked with all his strength. On the opposite shore, the wood anchored itself firmly with a satisfying *thunk*.

"Of course," muttered Newt.

"Now, Nathaniel," said Kieran, chewing back a grin, "don't go broodin' on this. There's nothin' wrong with ye' that a lot of good red meat won't cure." Newt glared at him, and Kieran tried to make amends. "So what do ye say we make use of this fine invention of yours? Who'll be the first to go across?"

Newt and Jori both stared into the icy river. Jori saw Newt's eyes narrow, and he looked back at Kieran suspiciously.

"Why not you?" he asked.

"Because, brother, that river looks hungry. Someone's got to stay on this side to hold the end of the rope."

Newt nodded reluctantly. "All right. Then I'll go first, and I can help pull Jori across." Jori bristled at the word *help*. But then she saw something in his face, and remained silent.

The river seemed to be climbing higher up the banks in anticipation. Waves crashed against the shore, then sucked themselves backwards. As Jori watched, Newt undid his belt and retied it around the rope, fashioning a kind of harness for himself.

She felt a sudden rush of fear. She ran over to Newt and clutched his arm.

"Be careful, okay? If you drown, I'm going to be really pissed." For the first time that day, Newt smiled.

Finally, teeth clenched, he slid down into the black waters, gasping in shock as the cold sliced into him. Kieran leaned backward, pulling the rope taut, and Newt grabbed it. Grimly, he began pulling himself across, inch by tortured inch. Jori was barely breathing.

And then it all went horribly wrong.

The river began howling, bubbling up around Newt and growing rougher with every foot he gained. Angry waves pummeled him, knocking him off his feet and giving him no time to draw a breath. Jori could see exhaustion and fear in his face, but he continued moving forward. And then the river, shrieking in fury, leaped over his head and swallowed him.

Jori fell to all fours on the riverbank.

"Pull, Kieran!" she screamed, and Kieran strained backwards until it looked as though the veins would pop from his arms. For an eternity of seconds, Jori could see nothing but the whirling black blood of the river. Finally, she glimpsed Newt's hand, still clutching the rope. He resurfaced, choking and gasping, and Jori sagged in relief.

He clung to the rope for a moment, fighting to drag air back into his lungs. Then he tightened his grip and once more started struggling toward the far bank.

His progress was hideously slow. A thick branch spun into him, smashing his ribs so that he doubled over in agony. But he slowly straightened up, positioned his upper arm to shield his bruised ribs, and continued his struggle until he was well past the halfway point.

And then he stopped.

Jori waited tensely, afraid that pain had finally overwhelmed him. But a moment later he reversed direction and started heading back toward them. The river immediately became less fierce, sank several inches on the banks.

He's decided not to leave, she thought in despair. She suddenly saw his lifeless form curled on the old man's floor, and she cried out over the muttering of the river.

"Newt! What are you doing? Keep going! Please!"

He ignored her, continuing toward them while spitting out mouthfuls of black water. Finally, he dragged himself back onto the bank and collapsed, chest heaving as he choked in huge gulps of air.

"Newt," she whispered, kneeling down next to him. "Why did you come back? You could have made it, if you'd wanted to."

"I know," he said, barely able to speak. "But you couldn't have."

"What?"

"The river would have killed you. I came back to help you get across."

Jori's throat tightened. "You're an idiot," she whispered.

"I know." He smiled. Nearby, Kieran stood watching them.

After Newt rested for a time, they prepared to risk the river again. Newt fashioned another rope harness for her, then slipped himself back into his own. Kieran grasped the end of the rope, and Jori and Newt slid into the river.

Jori gasped at the cold, her legs and hips becoming blocks of ice. She twisted her upper body quickly toward the rope so she could hold on with both hands. Newt positioned himself just behind her, stretching his long arms around her sides and placing his hands on the rope just next to hers.

"Are ye ready?" asked Kieran.

Newt tightened his grip. "As ready as we'll ever be."

"All right, then. Good luck."

They lumbered deeper into the river. Jori's heart almost stopped as the cold clamped her chest, and she shook so hard she thought her teeth would break.

"Don't worry," said Newt grimly. "It gets . . . worse."

He was right. Before they had moved even a few more feet, the river exploded in anger. Waves crashed over them, slamming them into the rocks and pouring into their mouths when they cried out in pain. Soon Jori was struggling for breath, her mind torn by terror. Once, she felt something ram into them from behind, and Newt groaned, his own body absorbing the worst of it.

Jori's hands were now blue, her face numb. More than once she slipped, and the river howled in triumph. But Newt always pulled her up again, holding tight until she regained her footing.

As they passed the halfway point, the river's fury increased. A harrowing moan spiraled from its depths, swirling around them like a living creature. A second voice joined the first, and then another, and another, until she and Newt were surrounded by a chorus of screams.

"Keep going," yelled Newt. "We're almost there."

Jori shook the water from her eyes and saw the branches of the dead tree reaching out with skeletal fingers. Newt lunged toward them, grabbing hold of nearest one. Then he tugged on Jori's wrist until she was able to grasp one, too.

They pulled themselves along the tree to the shore, where they fell into the mud and pressed their hands to their ears to block out the shrieks. The river hurled itself up the banks like a rabid dog, trying furiously to drag them back in.

Eventually, though, the screams died away. The river, defeated, hissed angrily and receded.

Jori lay curled next to Newt on the riverbank, dragging air into her burning lungs and waiting for the blood to stop thundering in her veins. Eventually, Newt struggled into a sitting position and helped her up next to him. She leaned forward onto her knees, still panting.

"Now we've got to get Kieran across," she said.

Newt didn't respond.

"Except I don't know how he's going to fight this current alone," she continued worriedly. "He held the rope for us. But he won't have anyone helping him."

Newt finally spoke, sounding somewhat distant. "Maybe he'll find something to tie that end to." Then he smiled, and his eyes met Jori's. "He should be smart enough to figure something out. After all, he's *my* brother."

They looked across to the opposite bank, where Kieran stood watching them. The river was still too loud for them to speak easily, but Jori stood and waved her arms urgently, signaling him to cross. For some reason, though, Kieran didn't respond. His eyes were fixed on Newt, and Newt, catching his gaze, slowly got to his feet. For a long moment, the two stood quietly, simply looking at each other.

Suddenly, Kieran grinned and waved back at them. Then he let go of the rope. The swirling current snatched it away and sucked it deep below the surface.

Jori froze in mid-wave.

"Kieran!" she cried. "What are you doing?"

Kieran cupped his hands to his mouth. "I've got to get back to William. And I'm thinkin' the two of ye don't really need me anymore."

Jori opened her mouth, but nothing more came out. On the other side of the river, Kieran raised his hand in farewell, and his eyes locked onto hers. She could see the crooked smile, and something tore inside her.

"Godspeed," he called.

Then he turned and strode away.

THIRTEEN

THE LAST PHAROAH

J ori and Newt stood silently on the riverbank, watching Kieran's figure grow smaller in the distance. Jori was swallowing so hard she thought her throat might crack.

She felt Newt's hand on her arm. "You okay?"

She didn't answer at first. Then she shook her head miserably.

"No. I'm not. I . . . thought he liked me."

Newt lifted his hand toward her face, then pulled back. "He does. Believe me, he does."

"Then why'd he go? Why didn't he come with us?"

Newt walked a short distance away, avoiding Jori's eyes. "Maybe it was because I didn't really want him to."

"You didn't . . . Why not?"

"Blame your wolf." Newt turned to face her. "Back in the glen, when we were attacked, I thought she was going to rip my throat out. Instead, she started talking. I could hear her voice in my head."

"What did she say?"

"A lot of things." He grimaced. "More than I wanted to hear. About this place, but mostly about me. She said I wasn't proving anything to anyone, not even to myself. And by the time she was done, I was thinking that maybe being here wasn't too good for me." He glanced at Jori. "Or for you, either."

"What are you talking about?"

"Before we ever reached the river, I had decided that I would try to go on with you. Without Kieran. I told him he could go back to the camp. Remember?"

Jori nodded slowly.

"But he didn't go back, Jori. And it wasn't me who was keeping him with us anymore."

Jori looked back across the river. "But if he hadn't been with us, we wouldn't have gotten across. We did need him."

Newt shook his head firmly. "No. I would've figured something out." He paused, his words seeming to surprise even him.

Jori sat down near the riverbank.

"It's just . . ." she said finally, "it's just that no one's ever wanted me before. Not the way I am now, anyhow."

"You think so?" said Newt, an odd expression on his face. "No one at all?"

"No one," said Jori. Her eyes filled again with tears.

Newt sighed, sat down next to her, and put an arm around her shoulders. "Don't worry," he said, giving her a light hug. "There'll be someone else who'll like you the way you are. I promise."

They sat silently for a long time, Newt not pressing Jori to talk to him, or even to continue their journey. Finally, though, he spoke.

"You were right, you know."

"About what?"

"About Derek and Marisa being here. He came back that day—the day you ran from the house. He had Marisa with him, and she looked like she wanted to kill him, screaming at him for dragging her to some crazy old house in an alley. Then Prof DePris took over. Told her how beautiful she was, how intelligent, how enchanting. And pretty soon she was telling him everything."

"What kind of everything?"

"All her dreams. About having it all, being admired. Maybe someday being this rich, powerful woman people would look up to. Prof. DePris just kept nodding, looking at her like she was the most amazing person he'd ever met.

"When she was done, he took her hand and told her how much she deserved all those things, and wasn't it too bad that there was no guarantee that she'd ever get them. Or that they'd last, even if she did. She didn't say anything else after that. A few minutes later, we were all up in the tapestry room, and I watched Derek wrap Marisa into his dream."

"His dream?"

"Yeah. Like you said, everything he does is for Marisa. The next thing I knew, they were gone, and I was here. And I didn't really care about them anymore." She saw his shoulders sag.

"It's okay, Newt," said Jori, forgetting her own misery for a moment. "How could you know what was really happening?"

"You knew," he said quietly. "And I think I did, too. But I wanted it anyway. Part of me still does." He smiled ruefully, then slapped his knees and pushed himself to his feet. "So. Maybe it's time the two of us stopped wallowing and got moving. What do you say?"

With some difficulty, Jori shoved away any remaining thoughts of Kieran. "I say you're right. No more wallowing."

They began walking, leaving the hungry black river behind. Within minutes, the desert sun scorched the clouds from a white-hot sky. Jori's lungs burned with every breath, and sheets of dust bit into her skin like a swarm of gnats.

She lifted her hands to block the sand. Something rippled across her cheeks, and she brought her fingers to her face. A loose cloth masked everything but her eyes.

She looked at Newt. He wore a long, light robe that reached almost to his ankles. Tough leather boots protected his feet, and yards of dyed material were wrapped around his head, mouth, and nose. From the way he was staring at her, Jori could only assume she wore a very similar outfit.

"Well," she said through the cloth, "I guess our other clothes were getting a little ripe."

"Oh, I don't know," said Newt, affecting a look of distaste as he plucked at his robe. "I sort of liked the tunic. Showed off my legs."

Jori laughed for the first time that day. After everything he'd been through, Newt was still Newt. And that reassured her, despite the blazing red rock around them. Maybe things really would get back to normal. Eventually.

A pillar of hot wind swirled around them, sucking at their garments. They began to struggle toward the hill they had seen from the river, heads down, scarves pulled tightly across their mouths. Just ahead of them, a horned adder whipped its way in graceful s-curves across the hot surface.

Jori wished she could move as easily as the snake. Instead, her boots sank into the burning sand whenever she leaned forward to take another step. Soon, every muscle in her shins and thighs throbbed with fatigue.

After what seemed like hours, they reached the base of a massive dune. Newt, who was about fifteen steps ahead of her, trudged a few feet up the side. He stopped and looked back, panting.

"This isn't going to be easy," he called. "It's like trying to climb up a mountain of ball bearings."

Jori began climbing, too, her body angled so far forward that she used her hands as much as her feet to struggle up the side. She slipped backwards every time she put a foot down, gaining only a few inches with each step. She wanted to scream with pain.

Newt finally struggled to where flat blades of red stone thrust up out of the sand. He pulled himself from rock to ridge, seeking out the surest and easiest paths. Jori followed closely behind. Finally, Newt neared the top, where the steep incline finally leveled off. A short distance away, the rock began to dip again, as though leading to some kind of valley.

"Wait here a second. Let me check it out first." He walked cautiously toward a narrow ledge that thrust out from the cliffs, straining to see what was in the valley beneath them. He stopped, and his mouth opened slightly. Then he waved Jori next to him.

She clambered onto the ridge and followed Newt's gaze.

Below them, the arid desert had surrendered its hold. In its place was a broad river delta, a miraculous expanse of rich black soil and golden fields of grain and corn. Not far away, Jori could see a busy harbor, with dozens of ships pulling into port or heading back out to see, and merchants trudging away from the docks with heavily laden mules.

Between the fields and harbor, a bustling city had grown. Jori could see hundreds of buildings—shops, stables, houses, and inns—and vendors haggling with their customers in a sprawling marketplace. Her eyes traveled slowly along the maze of streets, taking in every detail.

A large waterway bordered the far edge of the city, opening into a vast lake that fed into the harbor. In the center of the lake was an island, inclining gently upward until it formed a broad plateau. Near the top, eight white buildings glowed in the late-afternoon sunlight.

One structure, many times larger than the rest, shone like a crown at the highest point of the island. It appeared to be made of limestone and marble, supported by intricately carved columns and topped by elaborate towers, cornices, and statues. Adorning its grounds were landscaped ponds, hidden alcoves, and lush gardens draped with hanging vines, heavy with red and purple blossoms. The whole scene had the richness of an oil painting.

It looks like a palace, Jori thought, then realized it probably was. Encircling the island was a high defensive wall, broken only by a few gated doorways that opened onto the river. Outside the doorway nearest to them, Jori could see a magnificent river barge. It had purple sails and a gold canopy, and silver oars that sparkled in the late-afternoon sun.

Something flashed in Jori's memory.

"Alexandria."

"What?"

"This is Alexandria." She stared at the scene in front of her. "We watched a movie about it in World History. It was about the only time I didn't see Marisa text-messaging her way through class."

"And that was because . . . ?"

"Because this was the home of the Last Pharoah. The Queen of the Nile."

Newt looked blank.

"Cleopatra." Jori dredged up more facts. "She became Queen of Egypt when she was only seventeen. But that wasn't enough for her. She kept wanting more and more power. So she either seduced the men who could give her what she wanted, or murdered the ones that stood in her way. Even one of her brothers."

"I can see why Marisa would like her."

"Yeah. Anyhow, her palace was at Alexandria, by the Nile delta. And she'd sail up and down the river on a barge like that one, just so everyone could stare at her." Jori gazed at the boat, and at the massive white buildings. "I remember Marisa saying she'd like to go back in time and live her life."

"And Derek heard her."

"Well, he always sits right next to her." She paused. "So he really does care about her that much. Enough to build his whole dream around her." She shook her head in amazement. "I guess you never know what's going on inside a guy's head."

"No," said Newt, his voice a little odd. "Apparently not."

Jori heard the tone. But before she could ask what he meant, he stood and looked across the landscape. "So what do we do now? Go knock on the palace door and tell them it's time to go home? Somehow I don't think they'll be too receptive."

"No. So we've got to get to them some other way."

"Which means . . . ?"

"Flattery. Flattery will get you anywhere with Marisa."
Jori considered. "That, and jewelry. So let's go shopping."

★ ★ ★

They began picking their way down the rocky slopes, then
continued across the golden fields toward the harbor city.
Within an hour, they were in the center of the bustling
marketplace. Shops and stalls crammed every inch of space,
their owners haggling in a half-dozen different languages
with merchants streaming from the nearby ships.

Jori and Newt walked slowly through the streets, dizzy
with the thick salt smell of the sea and the aromas of a hundred strange spices. Unimaginable treasures sparkled on the
backs of mules and spilled from every stall. Jori stopped by
one vendor, transfixed by ropes of black pearls strewn
across his counter like strands of glistening seaweed. The
vendor saw her staring and lifted the pearls onto his arms,
sweeping them toward her.

"You like these, lady?" She nodded, mesmerized, and
the merchant shifted his eyes to Newt. "Then you must
buy them for her, sir."

Newt laughed. "Sure. Just as soon as I figure out where
I left my fortune."

He patted his thigh where there normally would have
been a pocket, then stopped in surprise. Jori looked down
and saw his hand close on a pouch tied around his waist, a

pouch that looked heavy with coins. Newt shook a few into his palm and looked at them curiously. Then he snorted.

"Check it out."

Jori peered over his shoulder. The coin was stamped with the image of a young woman. She was wearing elaborate jewelry and an ornate headdress, the kind Jori had seen in the Egyptian exhibits at the Natural History Museum. The face was beautiful, the bearing regal. But there was a haughtiness to the girl's expression, a slight sneer on her lips.

"Marisa," said Jori.

"No kidding."

A fanfare of trumpets sounded in the distance, from the direction of the island palace.

"What's that?" asked Jori, pressing one of the coins into the merchant's hand. The man bowed slightly, then raised his head.

"The Queen sets sail today. She and her consort."

Jori stared at Newt, and they began to run.

They reached the river's edge in minutes, their faces bright red and glistening with sweat. Across from them rose the massive wall surrounding Cleopatra's island, the top bristling with sharpened spikes, its broad expanse broken only by a single heavily guarded gate.

"Okay," said Newt. "So now all we have to do is get across the river, fight off the guards, figure out a way to get into the palace, score an audience with Mari-patra, and then convince her and Derek to give up a life of wealth and power."

Jori nodded. "Exactly."

Newt opened his mouth, but the trumpets sounded once more, just inside the walls of the island. The gate separated and swung inward, and a quartet of male slaves came through the opening, bearing a litter on which reclined a slim young girl.

"Or Marisa could just come to us," Newt murmured.

The slaves crossed onto the barge, trailed by four young women, and carefully set the litter on a raised platform. They lit two fire pots on either end of the barge, then positioned themselves at the prow and stern, where they stood like statues. The four handmaidens, meanwhile, knelt by Marisa's head and feet and on either side. They began feeding her fruit, fanning her, cooling her skin with moist cloths.

"Not so different than at school," Jori commented. "But I wonder where—"

Before she had even finished the sentence, a young man walked through the gateway with the arrogant swagger of a born commander. He wore the armor of a soldier but looked more Roman than Egyptian. Bands of hammered gold gleamed on each wrist, accenting lean, muscled arms. He strode onto the boat, and Marisa-Cleopatra raised one languid arm to beckon him to her. He moved swiftly toward the litter, just as the barge pushed away from shore.

Newt squinted as the boat drifted toward them. "So who's Derek supposed to be? Caesar? Or some kind of Mark Antony clone?"

Jori, too, was peering at the young man, who was now standing next to Marisa and stroking her hair. She started. "That's not Derek."

"What do you mean?"

"Just what I said. It's not Derek. It's someone else she's conjured up."

Newt leaned forward. "Shit. You're right. So what's happened to Derek?"

Jori never got to reply.

The ground beneath them began to shake, fragments of rock jittering madly at their feet. A deep rumble came from the south, from somewhere farther up the Nile, and Jori jerked her head to look.

Clouds boiled out of a black cauldron sky, their dark shadows swallowing the light. Color drained from the gardens, the white granite walls faded to gray, and the air turned dry and stale. Jori felt her skin grow cold.

"Newt," she whispered. "We've got to get out of here."

They tore back through the twisting streets, back toward the red mountains that encircled the city. Fear crawled across Jori's shoulders. She didn't dare look back.

Around them, the city staggered into stillness. The eager merchants halted in mid cry, their customers paralyzed around them. The streets began to shrivel, and the buildings lost their shape and texture. Jori and Newt raced out from among the shifting images and up the slopes of the surrounding mountains. Finally, as they neared the top, they turned and stared in horror at the dying city and its hideous shroud of clouds.

And then the Black River groaned out of the darkness.

Jori watched in horror as it snaked through the delta like a monstrous serpent, swallowing the waters of the Nile as it advanced, heaving itself onto the rich soil of the river-banks and crawling toward the city. There, it split into smaller streams and wound its way through the narrow streets, sending thin tentacles into each home, each shop, each dark corner. Looking for its prey.

Soon it reached the marketplace. Jori, straining her eyes toward the horrific sight, saw one thin liquid tendril lift itself from the current and seem to cast about for a scent in the air. It hesitated, then flowed over a group of merchants who stood unmoving outside one of the stalls. It briefly took on the shape of the men, and then the figures dissolved beneath it.

Now the river reached the far edge of the city and spilled into the lake, turning the mirror-bright waters to sludge. A moment later, it lurched out onto the island itself and Jori watched, unbelieving, as it begin to flow impossibly up the sloped sides, drawn to the island palace. Soon the beautiful ponds were gone, the brilliant gardens destroyed. The river entered the palace. A moment later, blood-red liquid streamed from every window.

Jori turned away, sick.

"What just happened?" whispered Newt.

"I don't know. I'm not sure. But maybe . . . maybe the river takes back the dreams, once they've started to fall apart. It was happening in Lisa's dreamscape too."

"But Marisa's dream was still fine. It looked like she had everything she wanted."

"It wasn't her dream."

She risked another look at the island. The waters were already receding, the Black River reversing its flow and heading out of the city. Back to wherever it came from.

"Come on," said Jori. They stumbled back down the hill, through the streets of the empty city, to the shore of the dead lake. The water was dark and stagnant, emitting a stench like a thousand corpses. Fish floated on the surface, filmed eyes staring. On the far shore, the barge lay smashed, its silver oars splintered like the broken legs of an insect. It was empty.

"It got her," Newt said dully. "We're too late."

"Maybe not," said Jori, trembling. "She may still be alive. Derek, too, since we didn't even see him here. But if they are alive, they'll probably end up wishing they weren't." Haltingly, she tried to explain about the dark center of the tapestry. About Maligor.

"It's where dreamers are taken when the fantasies aren't enough anymore. Or when they've stayed too long, and the dreams begin to twist into something else." She paused, finally allowing her mind to puzzle through what she hadn't wanted to realize. "And if the beautiful part of the tapestry was spun from dreams, then Maligor must be the opposite. Some kind of endless nightmare you can't wake up from."

Newt nodded, slowly. "I remember seeing the stain. But all I cared about was getting back into the tapestry."

Jori watched his expression shift from understanding to shock to horror. "So if you hadn't come after me . . ."

He stared at her. So how do I tell him the rest, she thought. She drew a deep breath.

"Newt. It's where I have to go now."

"Why? To get Derek and Marisa? Forget it. You've tried."

"No. I've got to go because that's where Lisa is."

For a minute, Newt didn't say anything. Jori saw a dozen emotions fight each other on his face. But then he stood a little taller, raised his chin slightly. "Well," he said. "I might as well come with you. Get my money's worth out of this amusement park."

Jori closed her eyes in relief. When she opened them, Newt smiled and nodded. But the furious muttering of the Black River continued in the distance, dragging their attention back to it.

"How do we get to the center, though?" Jori said. "We'll never get there on foot. And we can't travel on the river."

A voice came from behind them. "That is not quite true."

Jori spun around. Standing just a few feet away, motionless as stone, was a cadaverous man dressed in long dark robes. He was leaning on a tall wooden pole and smiling at them, his teeth green and broken. Sharp cheekbones stretched the gray skin of his face, and his bald skull was webbed with spidery blue veins.

"There is nothing to be afraid of," the gray man said, his voice like the whisper of dead leaves. "I am here to help you."

"Right," said Jori nervously. "In the way a snake helps a mouse."

"Clever girl." His rheumy eyes studied her, skittering across her face like roaches. Reminding her of something, or someone. "But your cleverness should not prevent you from listening to me."

"Why?"

"Because I'm your only way into Maligor." He bowed, then waved a hand toward the river. Drifting in the dark water was a long, flat boat, a ferry of some sort. It had two seats, front and back, and a place for the pilot to stand

"I can escort you down the River," the Boatman said, dipping his head. "As quickly or as slowly as you wish to travel."

"I'll bet you can," said Newt. "And what's to stop you from throwing us overboard?"

"Why would I do that? It is my great honor to take to Maligor any who wish to go. Any whom the River does not need to persuade."

Newt looked at Jori. "It makes sense," he said reluctantly. "Maligor wants us to come to it. Why not make it easier when it can?"

Jori nodded, equally unhappy with the logic.

"Excellent," purred the Boatman. "I can assure you that my service will be of the highest quality."

"That's great," said Jori, looking down the river. "First class travel . . . right into our nightmares."

FOURTEEN

MALIGOR

Jori and Newt sat stiffly in the gray man's ferry, watching the currents swirl past them like spilled blood. To Jori's surprise, the river stayed calm. But overhead, black clouds churned and boiled, a mirror of the river's dark soul.

Eventually they reached the main waterway, and the Boatman skillfully poled them into its currents. As they crossed the point where the two branches met, the landscape on either side changed dramatically. On their left was a sprawling lunar city, its bubble-shaped buildings silhouetted against a deep orange sky. On their right was a dense rain forest, resplendent with giant orchids, massive leather-leafed ferns, and trees that climbed hundreds of feet into the air. The huge skeleton of a dinosaur lay half in, half out of the water.

The Boatman's pole rose and fell, and the ferry slid silently down river. Hours, even days could have passed. Jori felt herself grow as still as the dead city they had left, hypnotized by the ever-changing dreamscapes. A floating island, supported by pillars of mist. A red dust-field, pockmarked with craters. A glimmering turquoise lagoon, its white sands strewn with shells. But each as lifeless as a painted backdrop.

"I don't understand," she said to Newt as a fortress of crystal and ice materialized in front of them. "Some of the tapestry was moving when we saw it. Some of these should still be alive."

It was the Boatman who answered, though, his voice crawling like a centipede across her skin. "After a time," he said, "nothing lives near these waters. Then the river itself must hunt for what it wants."

A violent roar ruptured the air. Jori jerked around. The river just ahead of them had disappeared, swallowed by a crackling red fog that blasted them with heat.

"What is that?" Jori gasped. "What's going on?"

Tongues of flame shot out of the mist, flicking across the river to lick at the ferry. Newt grabbed at the Boatman's robes. "What are you doing?" he shouted. "Push the boat to the shore!"

"There is no need," the Boatman grinned.

"No need? You're going to kill us! *Push the boat to shore!*"

The Boatman howled with laughter and shoved violently on his pole.

The inferno leaped toward them. Newt cried out, flinging his body over Jori's. She dug her fingers into his shirt, waiting for the agony of flames on flesh and the sound of their own screams.

Silence came instead. And no pain at all.

Can death come that fast? Jori wondered. Trembling, she raised her head.

The boat was gone, and the river had vanished. She and Newt were sitting on a tomb-like slab of rock, so cold it burned. Their long robes had disappeared, transformed once more into the clothes they'd been wearing when they first entered the tapestry.

Thick green mist smeared the darkness, and the stench of dead things hung in the air. Stark white trees caged them in, tortured skeletons rooted forever in the barren gray soil. Scuttling between their trunks were four-legged shadows, their red eyes gazing hungrily at the intruders.

A scream shattered the silence. Jori cringed, shrinking toward Newt. Three formless white shapes twisted from the trees and flew toward them, raising ghastly faces as they drew near. Their eyes and noses were hollow sockets; their mouths gaped wide in agony.

The specters seemed to be pleading with them, reaching out with nearly transparent arms. But their voices were no more than strangled moans. In frustration, they held their heads, tore at their own mouths. And then, gasping and sobbing, they slipped back through the trees and disappeared.

"What were those?" Jori whispered.

"I don't know," said Newt, his face pale. "I don't want to know, and neither do you."

No, I don't, thought Jori. But they seemed almost human. What if . . . her stomach dropped, and she fell to her knees.

"What is it?" Newt asked. "What's wrong?"

"What if those things are all that's left of the dreamers who came here? What if one of them was my sister?"

Newt stiffened, but just for a moment. He knelt next to her and grabbed her shoulders. "It wasn't Lisa," he said. "You would have known. You would have felt it."

But his words didn't reach her. A moan rose from her and she collapsed, sobbing.

A rabid growl ripped through the air, and Newt scrambled to his feet. Ragar stood just a few feet away, fangs bared, hackles raised. She snarled like a thing insane, then snapped at the air by Jori's face.

"Don't!" cried Jori, startled out of her anguish. "Ragar, stop! It's me!"

The wolf continued to growl, ears back, eyes fixed on Jori's face. But then her threatening posture relaxed, and her eyes grew calm. "I know who you are, girl."

"Then why—"

"Because you were giving yourself over to this place. Offering it exactly what it hungers for."

"I wasn't."

"You were. Despair is the most powerful weapon you can give to Maligor. It is what the creatures here feed on." She nodded toward the twisted trees, and one of the shadows darted forward, jaws snapping. A jackal.

Jori stared into the animal's hunger-mad eyes. Overwhelmed, she lowered her head. "I'm sorry. I'm just not strong enough to do this anymore."

"Yes you are," said Newt softly, and she raised her eyes to look at him. "You're stronger than anyone that I've ever known."

Ragar nodded approvingly. "He's right, girl. But you have suffered great loss, and great pain. A little weariness is to be expected. It doesn't change who you are . . . unless you allow it to."

The wolf's words, and Newt's quiet confidence, soothed Jori's wounded soul. She took a deep breath and straightened her shoulders. Ragar growled again, and the jackal slipped back into the shadows.

Jori looked at the wolf, silently asking for guidance.

"Now," said Ragar, "continue into Maligor. Search for your sister. And Jori—if you search long enough, you will find her." The wolf stepped forward and nuzzled her neck. Then she turned and loped away, fading into the green mist.

Jori closed her eyes, trying to pull together the shreds of her confidence, wishing she didn't feel quite so alone.

Without thinking, she whispered the first thought that entered her mind:

"Kieran. Please. I need you."

She opened her eyes, hoping. But she saw only Newt, a strange expression on his face. Disappointed and embarrassed, she looked away.

For a moment, neither of them spoke. But then she felt Newt move closer to her.

"You don't have to wish for Kieran, Jori. He's here."

Jori looked up, not understanding. But Newt leaned down, took her hands, and pulled her up beside him. His thin face was calm.

"You're not alone in this any more," he said softly. "I can be a hero, too."

Jori stared, not sure how to respond. But then images from their time together began to flash in her mind, from their harrowing passage across the river all the way back to the first time Newt had thrust himself between her and Marisa in the hallway of the school. Suddenly, to her amazement, she could see Kieran in every detail of Newt's face.

"I think you already are," she said.

Newt grinned in relief. "It's about time you noticed." And they stood together, quietly, for a long sweet time.

"So," Newt said finally. "Shouldn't we be going . . . somewhere?"

Jori looked around, trying to find some reason to choose one direction over another. Then she realized that where Ragar had vanished, the mist seemed to have parted, leaving wispy tendrils floating above what looked like a rough path. "That way," Jori said.

They started confidently down the trail, but soon it thinned, became lost under a thick mat of weeds and rotted black leaves. Jori and Newt continued to push forward, choosing whatever way looked least obstructed by the twisted trees and tangled vines. But they seemed to make no progress, wandering for hours with no sense of where they were going or where they had been.

And they could not relax, even for a moment. If they drew too close to the twisted trees, huge thorns thrust out from their trunks, sharp as dagger blades. And every few yards, hissing vines slithered down from above, dripping acid and trying to ensnare them. Worst of all, deep in the shadows, the jackals remained their unwanted escorts, lurking behind the trees, waiting for them to stumble.

Newt swatted at one of the squirming tendrils. "This is nuts," he muttered. "We could be walking in circles."

"I know." Jori kicked at the heads of small, sharp-beaked pods that snapped at her ankles, then crushed one with her shoe, smiling grimly as she heard it squeal. "At this rate, we'll never find anyone."

A sound like a pistol shot cracked the air, and the ground quaked and rolled. Jori grabbed frantically for Newt's arm, twisting toward the sound. In the distance, on the edge of a vast plain, a monstrous mass of black rock heaved and shuddered. Its jagged peaks slashed through a boiling bank of clouds, and dark streams of water erupted from cracks in its surface, spilling down the sides like endless gouts of blood.

The Black Rivers, she thought. *This is where they come from.*

A red glow burst from the scarred cliffs, and long shadows reached across the plain with cold, black fingers. They slid toward Jori, grasping at the thorn trees and melting into dark blotches that pockmarked the ground. *What are those*, Jori wondered, then realized they were open pits, dozens of them, gaping like hungry mouths. Low moans and cries spiraled around her, but she couldn't tell whether they came from inside the holes or were voiced by the cold wind blowing across them.

"They look like traps," Newt said. "The kind hunters use to catch large animals."

"Or people." Jori stared at the pits, an awful certainly taking hold. "She could be here, Newt."

A loud hiss came from above them.

A spidery figure dropped from the branches of the tree next to them, landing in a tight ball on the ground. It swiftly unwound its long limbs and pulled itself erect, towering over Newt by more than a foot, swaying back and forth on pole-like legs. Black and purple scales sheathed most of its body, but the chest and stomach were pale yellow, like a lizard's underbelly.

"Ah, jeez," said Newt, quickly pulling Jori behind him. "I picked a great time to be a hero."

Jori barely heard him, transfixed by the apparition in front of them. It lowered its head and examined them, eyes glowing orange, mouth stretched in a permanent grimace. Newt tried to retreat, but the thing snatched at his clothes, long talons clacking. Newt swung at its arm, and it threw back its head and screeched.

Three more of the creatures dropped from the thorn trees, so close that Jori could smell their sour breath, see needle-sharp teeth jutting from their gums. Their eyes slid from Jori to Newt, then back again.

"Are they freshhhh?" one whispered, staring at Jori.

Its companions sniffed at the air and licked their lips. "Quite freshhhh," said the one who had first appeared. "Quite new."

"Can they be takennnnn?"

"Easssily."

There was a low hum of excitement.

And then they sprang.

Jori screamed, caught in a tangle of cold arms and sharp claws. The creatures shrieked in triumph as they lifted her into the air and hurled her into one of the hideous black holes.

Dead roots whipped at her as she fell, gouged her when she hit bottom. Gasping at the pain, she flung her arms over her head, expecting the creatures to leap down and rip her to pieces.

Nothing happened. She lowered her arms and straightened her bruised body. She tried to find Newt, but darkness shuttered her eyes.

A groan came from her right.

"Newt! You okay?"

"I'm not sure."

Jori dragged herself toward him, reaching out blindly. She touched cloth and found him struggling to sit up. "I'm all right," he said finally, fumbling for her hand. "Are you?"

"I think." She finally found the courage to look upward. At first, all she could see were snarled clumps of weeds silhouetted against the glowing green mist. An instant later, the faces of their captors appeared overhead, grinning down at them.

"Who are you?" she whispered. "What do you want?"

The creatures gnashed their teeth, flexed their long claws. One leaned farther over the edge, into the pit itself.

"We are Horridins," it said, its voice like broken glass. "But that doesn't matter. Not to a humannn. Not for long."

"What are you going to do to us?"

"Do?" hissed another, baring its piranha's teeth. "Nothing, human. Not now. But here we will leave you. Two days, three. However long it takes for fear to fill your veins and soften your bodies. And thennn—then we will feed."

Jori's stomach cramped, and a small whimper escaped her. The Horridins grinned.

"Good," one murmured. "It has already begun."

Jori heard a strangled cry, and the creatures looked up in alarm. A giant claw whipped through the air, knocking one of the Horridins from view. The others screeched, leaping back from the edge of the pit. Dull thuds and sharp cracking sounds echoed down to where Jori and Newt clung to each other, and the Horridins' shrieks swelled into howls of agony.

Abruptly, the sounds stopped. All Jori could hear was the dry rustle of something scurrying away.

"What's going on?" asked Newt tensely. Then a stream of dirt trickled over the edge of the pit.

A face appeared, filthy and wild-eyed. And human.

Jori's jaw dropped. "Who are you?"

The face pulled back.

"Wait," she called frantically. "Come back! You've got to get us out of here!"

The face appeared again, staring down at them. But then it vanished a second time.

"Please! Whoever you are. You can't just leave us!"

For a minute, she heard nothing. Then there was a scraping sound, and the end of a long branch appeared over the hole. It teetered on the edge, then slid downward and struck the bottom of the pit. The huge thorns jutting from its side were sharp as knives—but their thick bases also formed a solid, makeshift ladder.

Newt nodded toward the branch. "Go ahead. I'll hold it steady." He positioned his hands firmly around the trunk.

Jori grasped the thick ends of two of the thorns and tested a lower one with her foot. It held. Fixing her eyes on the edge of the pit, she climbed toward the green mist.

When she reached the top, she peered over the edge, afraid that the Horridins might be waiting nearby. But all she saw was a still figure, huddled under a thorn tree a short distance away. One hand rested on a long, thick branch—the claw that had snatched the first Horridin.

She clambered the rest of the way out and took a step in their rescuer's direction, raising her hand in thanks. But whoever it was didn't react at all, even though the eyes seemed to be staring directly at her.

Jori's arm dropped back to her side. A moment later, Newt pulled himself from the hole and walked over to her. They both looked at the person by the tree, who remained unnaturally, frighteningly still.

Jori moved closer. Finally, she was able to make out dark hair beneath the filth, and a lean frame shivering under strips of torn brown leather. Green eyes stared dully through the mud.

"Derek," she whispered.

She ran to him, crouched down, tried to warm his cold hands between hers. But there was no response. "Derek, you okay? It's us. Jori and Newt."

Newt hurried up beside her, looking troubled. "He helped us. Why would Derek help us?"

"I don't know. But he did." She stared into the other boy's empty eyes, felt his thin fingers. "He looks so sick," she said worriedly. "Newt, what if helping us used up whatever strength he had left? What happens to him then?"

The answer screamed out of the pits behind them. Jori turned and saw two Horridins scuttling away, one dragging a hand across its wet lips. Behind them, a transparent white shape, vaguely human, rose from the hole. Moaning in grief, it looked down at the vapor that was now its body. Then it drifted off into the woods, sobbing.

A moment later, the jackals arrived.

Newt grew pale. "That's what we saw when we first got to Maligor. This is where they came from."

"So if we hadn't gotten out . . ." She looked back at Derek. His blank stare had been replaced by a look of stark terror, and he was trembling.

"Derek, can you hear me?" she asked, squeezing his hands again. "We've got to get out of here. Before they come back."

His voice suddenly cracked from his throat. "No," he said, shaking his head violently. "*No, no, no, no, no!*" He wrenched his hands from Jori's grip and leaped to his feet, stumbling away from her. Newt leaped forward and grabbed him by both arms.

"It's okay, Derek! They're not here. It's okay!"

"No!" shrieked Derek. "You're not going to get me this time!" He kicked at Newt, struggling to free himself.

"Derek," Newt shouted, shaking him roughly. "Derek, you ass! Quit fighting me!"

Jori's jaw dropped. But Derek froze, his eyes fixed on Newt's. For a moment, they stood locked in position.

Derek swallowed. "Newt?"

"Yeah. It's Newt."

Derek turned his gaunt, filthy face to Jori.

"It's us, Derek. Really."

He didn't move. But finally he let out a long, shuddering breath, and some of the panic left his face. Slowly, Newt released his arms, watching tensely in case he tried to run again.

Derek passed a trembling hand over his eyes. "I thought maybe I was imagining you. I thought this place had messed up my mind again." He stared at Jori desperately. "You're sure you're real?"

"I'm sure. Come on. Let's rest for a minute."

She gently led Derek back to the thorn tree where he had been sitting, and the three of them huddled together on the icy ground. Derek looked at the other two, unblinking, as though afraid they might vanish if he closed his eyes.

"Derek," said Newt. "Where did you come from? We didn't see you when we first got here."

"I was in one of the holes," he whispered, his eyes straying back to the barren field. "Just like you were."

"And Marisa?" Newt asked. "What about her?"

Derek was silent.

"Derek?"

"I haven't seen her."

"But you must have looked for her when you first got here."

"No. I didn't." He wouldn't look at them. "I mean, why should I? Back where we were, in the palace, she told me I was useless, that she was sick of me. Wouldn't even let me come near her."

"Classic Cleopatra—or Marisa," Jori said quietly, a bitter edge to her voice. "Either one uses you, then dumps you when she doesn't need you anymore."

Derek didn't seem to be listening. "It was eating me up," he said. "I kept trying to give her things, do things for her. Just like back home. But she just got angrier. Finally, she had me thrown in some kind of cell, under the palace. I heard a guard saying I'd be there forever—that I'd rot there." He paused. "That's when the River came."

Jori ached at the pain in Derek's voice.

"It spit me out here, like a piece of garbage. I wandered around for a while, trying to find some way out. But then I gave up. And before I knew what was happening, the Horridins grabbed me."

His face twisted, and he began to rock back and forth. "There were five of them, maybe six. They threw me down in the hole, and then just kept shrieking, spitting on me. Finally, one leaned over the edge, drooling. He said that they were leaving, but that they'd be back for me soon. And then they disappeared.

"After that, all I could hear were moans and screams, coming from all around. Pretty soon I just wanted it all to be over. So I just sat there, in the dark. Waiting for them to come back and finish me."

Jori felt a chill that had nothing to do with the wind. What would it have been like, she thought, curled up alone at the bottom of that pit, waiting for death to come grinning over the edge? She spoke softly.

"At least you got out before they did come."

The blood drained from Derek's face. "No. I didn't."

"What do you mean?"

"They didn't wait long. I don't know if it was just a few hours, or maybe a few days, but then they were back. Crawling over the edge, down to where I was." Tears began to spill from his eyes, and he rubbed his hands angrily across his face. "Two of them grabbed my shoulders and slammed me against the side of the pit. The others crouched on either side of me. I felt their teeth go into my arms and then . . . they drank." He raked his nails through his hair as though trying to claw away the memory.

Horror clamped itself around Jori's chest, and Newt looked sick. "But you're alive," he whispered.

Derek shut his eyes. "They told me they never come just once. That it would get better and better, the more afraid I was." He choked back a sob. "And oh, shit, I was very afraid."

Newt shuddered, then leaned over and gripped the other boy's shoulder.

"Yeah, but you didn't let it happen. You got out." He paused. "What finally made you try?"

Derek opened his eyes. "You guys did."

"What?"

"I was lying at the bottom of the pit, too sick to even move. After a while, I thought I heard the Horridins again, and all I could think about was how I could kill myself before they did. But then I heard voices. Yours."

Jori remembered. It was when she and Newt had first seen the pits.

"All of a sudden, I thought that maybe if I could just get out . . . I felt around the side of the pit, and there was a dead root or something sticking out from the dirt. I grabbed it and climbed up the side." His eyes dimmed. "When I got to the top, the first thing I saw was the Horridins attacking you. I heard you scream. And I finally just lost it, I guess."

"Lucky for us," said Jori softly.

A haunted expression crossed Derek's face. "Maybe. But then I wasn't sure of anything anymore. I'd been imagining so many things, down in the dark." He hesitated. "And I didn't think I could stand to find out if you were real or not."

Jori placed her hand on his torn, blood-smeared arm.

"We're real, all right," she said softly. "And we're not going anywhere without you." His face crumpled, and he jerked away. She quickly changed her tone. "That is, if you can manage not to be a *complete* idiot this time around. Any chance of that?"

Derek remained motionless for several seconds. But then he nodded.

FIFTEEN
SWAMP HAG

Derek sat silently for a long time, staring at nothing. Slowly, the haunted look left his face. But still he didn't speak.

"Derek," Jori said finally. "You okay?"

He shivered slightly, as though brushed by a cold hand. "I should've been dead by now."

Jori exchanged a worried look with Newt. If Derek's mind kept taking him back to the pit, he'd be as lost as if he'd never escaped it. The best thing to do, she decided, was to get him focused on something else, something far away from the sight of the yawning pits.

"Listen," she said. "I think it's time we got moving. I don't know where Lisa is, but I'm not going to find her by sitting here."

Derek flinched, pulling his wounded arms to his chest. "No. I just want to get out of—" He stopped, his voice dropping. "Your sister's here?"

She nodded. "I found her things at the old man's house."

Derek swallowed, then stared out at the bleak plain. Finally he muttered something and pushed himself to his feet. "Okay," he whispered. "Okay. Let's go find her."

What do you know, thought Jori. Not pond scum at all.

They moved cautiously across the howling landscape. Derek kept his eyes fixed on the ground, but Jori and Newt searched each death trap they passed, hoping to find someone else still alive.

All they saw, though, were grisly reminders of what the holes once held. Torn clothes at the bottom of one. A partial skeleton in another, one hand reaching toward the top of the pit. Finally, they stopped, unable to keep looking—it was too much like peering into open graves.

The mountain shuddered again. Without saying a word, all three turned and began heading directly toward it. They wandered for hours, the eternal gloom of Maligor freezing their bones. Jori shivered constantly, tortured by images of what might be happening to Lisa. Little by little, she took refuge in a part of her mind where she couldn't see what was around her, couldn't feel, couldn't think. She stayed there for a long time.

Abrupt flashes of light startled her out of her trance. She blinked, then saw a dozen brilliant veins of color slicing through the ground from every direction. She stared at them, knowing that she couldn't have seen them before, yet positive that she had.

She froze.

"Newt! Derek! I know how to find Lisa!" They spun toward her. She pointed to one of the threads, a deep sapphire one, and traced its path to where it converged with another, then another. They all headed in one direction— toward the bleeding mountain.

"Those are the tapestry threads. And Lisa's at the other end of one of them."

"You sure?" asked Newt.

"Pretty sure. Because you were right, Newt. I don't think she's dea—" She glanced at Derek. "I don't think she's around here. Part of her dreamscape was still alive, and it wasn't the River that pulled her away from it. She went off on her own."

Newt gazed at the hulking mountain. "Well," he said, taking a deep breath, "I guess we all knew we'd be dealing with that thing sooner or later."

Jori felt a twinge of guilt.

"Newt. Derek. You don't have to do this. She's my sister, not yours. Why don't you two—"

"Forget it," Newt said. "We're not going to stop watching out for each other now."

She smiled gratefully, then saw Derek watching them, his eyes mirroring still-raw emotions.

"What about you?" she asked. "Can you can handle this?"

"Do I have a choice?" He forced a smile. "I'll be okay. Like Newt said, I guess we're watching out for each other, now. I mean, I know he was just talking to you, but—"

"Shut up, moron," Newt said. He threw a light punch at Derek's shoulder. "It's all of us."

Derek nodded. "Well, all right then."

★ ★ ★

They now moved quickly across the barren landscape, Jori more hopeful than she'd been since she entered the tapestry. At least now she knew what to do, where to go. And she believed what she had told Newt. Lisa was still alive. All they had to do was find her.

As they traveled, Newt attempted to raise Derek's spirits with a rambling monologue about anything that wasn't important. The perils of cafeteria food. The inherent dangers of regular exercise. And, most tragically, the unarguable fact that the girls in school never looked like the ones you saw on TV.

"Yeah," said Derek finally. "Why is that? They've got to come from somewhere."

"They do," said Newt somberly. "From another solar system. Every so often, a spaceship lands somewhere on earth and deposits another batch of pods. Most of them in California."

"I guess that makes sense."

"Of course it does. There's no other explanation."

Jori joined in. "But why are they being sent here? Why not keep them . . . wherever?"

Newt considered. "I suspect it's to undermine us, soften us for an impending invasion. I mean, think of all the kings and presidents that have been victimized by these creatures."

Derek nodded. "It's also a good explanation for Marisa."

Newt and Jori laughed, and Derek grinned. What do you know, Jori thought. He's going to be okay. Impetuously, she threw her arms around him and kissed his cheek. He looked at her, startled.

"Whoa. What was that?"

She shrugged, laughing. "I'm not sure. About a week ago, I only would have done that in some sick, twisted nightmare."

Derek smiled, but then looked around at the howling landscape. "So I guess things haven't really changed that much."

Jori suddenly realized she was no longer cold. The air around them had grown warmer, more humid, and the sterile plain had disappeared. In its place were acres of soggy marshland and clumps of rigid stalks topped with sharp brambles. Trees again loomed over them, but these were giants with thick, multi-columned trunks and long branches that sent shoots plunging back into the earth.

Thick ropes of sap oozed steadily from each limb, as though the trees were melting.

Jori's fragile optimism vanished. Without speaking, she and the boys pulled closer together.

Now the mud became a stagnant pond, pockmarked with algae. On the surface of the water, oily globules formed like boils, then burst, belching out a thick sulphurous stench. Tiny black dots buzzed in Jori's ears and bit into her skin, leaving streaks of blood mixed with sweat. And from the darkness came the nerve-wracking whisper of things creeping nearby and unseen.

A rickety walkway rose from the scum, and they clambered onto it. Jori stared straight ahead, balancing carefully. But out of the corner of her eye, she could see the glistening skin of some large creature slithering just beneath the surface, near the pathway.

"We've got to get out of here," whispered Newt from behind her. "This is trouble waiting to happen."

"He's right," said Derek. "We should—"

His voice gasped into silence as suddenly as if his throat had been slit. Turning, Jori saw him looking down, his face white. She followed his gaze. Clutching Derek's ankle was a long green hand.

The swamp around them began to bubble and steam. Dome-like skulls rose slowly from the muck, and soon a dozen grotesque faces peered up at them, their eyes just breaking the surface. More hands flashed out of the water, snatching now at Jori and Newt.

"Get away," snapped Jori, crushing a grasping set of claws under her heel.

The thing shrieked, writhing in pain. It rose partway from the water, and Jori could see a green-skinned hag with a wide, lipless mouth. Strands of seaweed hung from her head instead of hair, and two flaps of skin puffed in and out in the center of her face, like gills.

The hag spat at Jori and dove beneath the surface. The others followed immediately, and Derek was yanked off the walkway. The swamp closed over him, and Jori could see his terrified eyes staring up at her through the water. The hag who held him shot forward, streaking away from them.

"Come on!" screamed Jori. She and Newt tore along the walkway, following the rise and fall of the hags' wet bodies. Occasionally, Jori could see Derek as well, thrashing in the water and gasping for air.

They finally reached the muddy bank of what seemed to be an island rising from the middle of the swamp. Jori watched as Derek was pulled from the water and up the side of the island, toward another hag who sat on a massive pile of dirt and wet vines. The creature who held him slouched to the very top, then violently threw him down at the other's feet.

The thing on the mud pile leaned over, eyes sharp with interest. Her neck and limbs were thin as twigs, and her ribs heaved under the mottled skin of her torso. Her long black hair, caked with mud, was braided with cracked bits of shell and bone. She sniffed Derek's neck, then jerked backwards, grimacing.

"How dare you!" she hissed. "How dare you show your face after deserting me!"

Jori heard Derek's horrified voice.

"Marisa?"

Jori's eyes darted to the creature's face. It was Marisa— or a hideous caricature of what the girl had once been. The monster grinned, plucking delicately at Derek's hair with bony fingers.

"Fortunately for you, I am not vindictive. Have you come seeking forgiveness?"

Jori's old anger exploded inside her, and her hands knotted, so desperately did she want to throttle Marisa. As if in response, a thin ramp materialized at the end of the walkway, stretching over to the island. Jori stormed onto it, and Marisa's head snapped up. She jerked forward eagerly, her fingers digging into Derek's scalp.

Jori stopped. This wasn't going to help Derek. It wasn't going to solve anything. She forced a benign expression onto her face. "Marisa. What's going on? What do you think you're doing?"

The thing smiled, exposing sharp teeth. "What does it look like?"

"It looks like you're sitting on a pile of mud with garbage in your hair."

The attendant hags shook with rage, and Marisa's face went dark. She released Derek, who dragged himself a few feet away. "Still blind with jealousy, aren't you?"

Jori's jaw dropped. "Jealousy? Are you—" She forced herself to remain calm. "No, I'm not jealous. I just think that maybe it's time we got out of here. All of us."

Marisa looked at her as though she were crazy. "Out? Why would I want to leave?"

"So you could go home. To everything you've—" Jori hesitated, then swallowed the remnants of her own hurt and pain—"everything you've accomplished there. And all your dreams of what you were going to have."

The creature's face became stone. "And that's all they were. Dreams. The old man was right. There were no guarantees out there, and whatever I did get could have disappeared in a month, or a day. But this," her arm swept the island, "This is all mine, and this will last forever."

Jori blinked, suddenly understanding. Marisa wasn't seeing where she was. She was seeing what Maligor wanted her see. As far as Marisa knew, she was still a queen, living on her island palace.

"Marisa, listen to me. You're not Queen of the Nile anymore. Can't you see where you really are? What this really is?"

Marisa stared at her, resisting, but Jori steadily held her gaze. Finally, Marisa's eyes left Jori's face and began flickering over her surroundings. At first, she nodded, her expression smug and satisfied. But then she blinked, and her smile faltered and faded.

Jori leaned toward her.

"You're seeing it, aren't you Marisa?" The girl didn't respond, but her face began to contort, horror chasing away the satisfied smirk.

"So come on, Marisa. Come back with us. You can still have everything you wanted—"

"No!" shrieked Marisa, lashing out wildly. "You're trying to trick me. I knew you would! You want me back the way I was. A nothing. A nobody!"

"No, that's not—"

"Get away from me. Get away, *you scarred freak!*" She lunged forward, slashing at Jori with her claws.

"Marisa, stop! Leave her alone!"

It was Derek. He stood trembling before the pile of mud, arms outstretched, his face pleading with the girl who shook and snarled in front of them. "Leave her alone. Please." Marisa drew back, her eyes narrowing as she stared at Derek. "She's right, Marisa. You have to come with us. I'll do anything you want. I'll even leave you alone for the rest of your life if you just do this one thing for me."

The shreds of panic left Marisa's face, and her head tilted thoughtfully. "You really do love me, don't you?"

Her voice was an incongruous purr in her disfigured face. Derek stared at her.

"Yes."

"You worship me."

He nodded, shaking.

"Then stay here, with me," she said, leaning toward him. "You want to, don't you?"

Derek hesitated. When he answered, his voice was a whisper. "Yes."

Shocked, Jori stared at Derek. He was as lost in the nightmare as Marisa. She grasped his arm.

"Don't listen to her, Derek. Don't let her suck you down with her!"

But Derek was already reaching for Marisa's claw.

Newt leaped out past Jori, shoving her to the side. He grabbed Derek, yanking him from Marisa's grasp. She fell to the ground, shrieking.

Two of the hags lunged at Newt. One whipped her long arm into his face and sent him reeling backwards. The other sprang on top of him, beating at his chest and stomach with wiry claws. Jori leaped forward, digging her nails into one of the hag's bony shoulders. But its muscles seemed made of iron.

"Enough!" shrieked Marisa. The hags froze. When Marisa spoke again, her voice was flat.

"You aren't worth the effort," she said, then looked directly at Derek. "Any of you." She raised her hand and beckoned to her attendants. "Dispose of them," she commanded. "And never let anything like them near me again."

Before Jori could move, she was grabbed around the neck and dragged into the cold green water. The muck pushed into her nose and mouth, and she clawed frantically toward the surface. But only seconds later, she was tossed up onto a mud bank, choking and gasping, like a piece of refuse. When she looked up, she saw only a bony green back disappearing beneath the surface.

She heard harsh breathing next to her and turned to find Newt pushing his wet hair out of his eyes. Derek was sitting a short distance away, his head lowered, his fingers digging into his thighs. The anguish on his face tore at her.

"Derek. Listen. There was nothing we could do."

"I know," he said, his voice so low that Jori could barely hear him. "But I did this to her. Me."

"What are you talking about?"

"Back home, you think I didn't know she was getting sick of me? I'm stupid, but not that stupid. I dragged her into the tapestry so I wouldn't lose her." His voice sounded strangled. "Look what I did to her instead."

Jori pulled herself toward him. "Derek, it's not your fault, any more than it's mine. Maybe you brought her here, but what you gave her was beautiful. She's the one who ruined it."

"But—"

"She would've let you rot, back at that palace. You had to know that. That's why she didn't end up in one of those pits when she got here, like the rest of us. Maligor knows who it needs to destroy, and who's already become a part of it."

Derek sat quietly for a few minutes, his forehead on his knees. Finally, he lifted his head. "Maybe you're right. Still, I wish I knew for sure."

"Nothing's for sure in this place," said Newt. "Except maybe one thing."

"What?"

"You were way too good for her, man."

Derek looked at him, startled. Then a ghost of a smile crossed his face. "Yeah. Maybe I was."

SIXTEEN

BLOOD MOUNTAIN

The swamp now seemed eager to be rid of them, subtly removing the obstacles that had blocked their way. With every step they took, the vegetation grew less dense, the ground more solid. The thick-limbed trees seemed to shrivel, then vanished altogether as though sucked back into the earth. Only shadows remained, and the steady pulse of the distant mountain.

A thin shaft of red light pierced the gloom, strobing across the landscape. It streaked across the ground to where

Jori and the others stood, then slowly rose again, delicately tracing their bodies.

Jori lifted her eyes and saw that the beam emanated from the highest peak of the mountain. It's watching us, she thought. Seeing if it's broken us yet. She lifted her chin defiantly, then motioned to Newt and Derek. They nodded, and the three of them headed once more toward the brooding black giant.

An hour or so passed, and Jori ran her tongue across dry lips. If only the heat would let up. But the air just became hotter, drier, almost scorching the skin from her body. Even the ground was parched, a cracked red plain on which nothing moved and no plants grew. At least there's no place for anything to hide, Jori thought, and she relaxed slightly, allowing herself a brief respite from thinking or worrying or speaking.

Newt and Derek took up the slack. Despite the heat, the two were soon deep in conversation, and Jori hung back a bit, letting the friendship take root. At one point, she saw Newt put a hand around his own neck and pretend to strangle himself. Derek bent over with laughter. Jori shook her head.

Eventually Newt stopped and waited for her.

"You know," he said, pushing a few strands of sweat-drenched hair from Jori's forehead, "I was just saying to Derek that risking death, dismemberment, and ingestion by monsters makes for great entertainment, but most people just go to the movies when they're bored. How about it? Maybe we can still score some cheap tickets at a matinee."

"Sure," she said. "If I can have the jumbo popcorn." But then Newt's face seemed to melt in front of her, and her heart began pounding against her chest.

"Jori. You okay?"

"I'm not sure." A wave of dizziness rolled through her head, then curdled her stomach. "Maybe not." A moment later, her knees buckled. Newt and Derek grabbed her arms and eased her gently to the ground.

"It's this damn heat," Newt said. "And everything else catching up with you. Let's just rest here a while, okay?"

"Okay." Jori leaned forward, propped her head on her knees, and tried to stop her brain from spinning. She sensed Newt crouching next to her, felt his hand gently stroking her hair.

"That feels nice," she murmured.

His hand left her head.

"Newt? Why'd you stop?"

There was no answer. She lifted her head, looked around in confusion. All she saw was the empty plain and a dark, throbbing sky.

"Newt? Derek? Where are you?"

Still no response. Trembling, she rose to her feet. She took a few unsteady steps, and the red beacon struck her face, blinding her. Shielding her eyes, she looked up toward the mountain. It was watching her. Waiting. She felt a rush of dread, and her voice scraped from her parched throat.

"What have you done with them?"

The light left her face, moved off behind her. She turned slowly, and her heart lurched.

No. This couldn't be. The holes hadn't been there before, she would have seen them. But now she heard cries and gasps from all around her, rising from an endless field of gaping black pits.

She was back in the plain of the Horridins.

"No," she whispered. "Please, not here. Don't let them be here. Derek'll die if those things come for him again. And Newt . . . Newt . . ."

She heard a moan from the pit just ahead of her, and lunged toward it. Falling to her knees she looked over the edge.

And began screaming.

"Jori! Jori, wake up!"

She gasped, eyes snapping open, and found Newt clutching her shoulders, his face white. Derek stood behind him, equally shaken.

"Jeez, Jori! You okay?"

For a moment she didn't answer. Then, slowly, she nodded.

"Yeah. Yeah, I'm okay. Only . . ." She looked from one to the other. "I thought you'd been taken, that you were back in the pits. I saw you at the bottom of one. You were both—" She looked at Derek, who nodded, almost imperceptibly.

"But we're not," said Newt. "We're here."

"I know. But . . ." She shivered violently. "Look. We've got to stay together, okay? We're only strong enough to fight this place if we stay together."

"You kidding?" said Newt, trying to calm her. "I'd take you in a bet against Maligor any day." Jori didn't smile. "Okay, okay. We'll stick like glue."

The ground muttered beneath them.

"Shit," said Derek. "Look over there."

The landscape was changing again. Pushing up from the plain were razor-sharp ridges and jagged fingers of stone, scraping against each other to form a brutal phantasmagoria of burning red rock. The ground shrieked and sobbed as it split apart, steam hissing through the fissures. Through the twisted formations, the jeweled tapestry threads darted like rivulets of fire.

Jori stared, willing herself to see past this newest barrier, trying once more not to lose hope. She shut her eyes, pictured Lisa at the other end of one of the gleaming strands, waiting patiently for her. When she finally opened her eyes again, Newt was watching her.

"We'll find her, you know."

"I know." She forced a smile, then took a deep breath. "You guys ready?"

Derek raised an eyebrow. "We are. Are you?"

"I'm fine. Let's go."

They picked their way over the ridges and between the giant stone columns, following the glowing tapestry coils through the dark forest of rock. Sharp protrusions on the stone slabs sliced their arms and legs as they climbed, and the scalding heat raised quick blisters on their hands.

Near the edge of the maze, the ground sloped steeply upwards, forming a final wall that separated them from the mountain. As they climbed, Jori's exhaustion began to overtake her once more, sapping her small reserves of energy. Newt motioned to Derek, and they moved slightly ahead, searching out the easiest paths.

Finally they neared the top of the incline, and Newt and Derek paused, waiting for her. She reached the top only to find that an equally torturous path lay before them. The rough slope down was covered in slabs of broken rock and shifting streams of sand. It led into a shadowed canyon that gradually opened up again at the base of the dark mountain.

"Come on," she said, and started down.

The earth shrieked.

A violent tremor rattled Jori's bones and the ground lurched, throwing her off her feet. Fissures blew open, and jagged trenches cracked the earth like lightning. One streaked toward Jori, splitting on either side and isolating her on a crumbling tower of rock. Her fingers scrabbled at the ground as Newt slid down the incline toward her.

"Grab my hand!" he yelled. But the void separating them was already too wide.

A huge stone slab jutted up between them, pushing itself into the air high over Jori's head. Over the shrieking of the rocks, she heard Newt cry out her name. Before she could answer, the stone tower collapsed. She was swept away on an avalanche of dirt and stone.

The rocks roared downward, flattening bushes and crashing against the walls that continued to erupt around her. Jori fought desperately against the river of stone, terrified she would be buried alive. Finally, the ground leveled off. She slammed up against a dead thorn tree and threw her arms around it, sobbing and choking on the dust. She felt blood dripping down the right side of her face, her scars ripped open and raw.

The thunder of rock faded, replaced by an eerie silence. Jori stood, heart pounding, and screamed for Newt and Derek. No one answered.

Just like in her dream.

The mountain loomed over her, its caves glowing like a thousand spiteful eyes, the pulsing red light forming an obscene halo around its peaks. From the gashes in its sides thundered the streams of the Black Rivers, roaring over the rocks toward the endless decay of Maligor

She saw a flicker of movement above her. Jackals crawled out of the shadows, their crooked silhouettes prowling over the mountain's broken face. They stared down at her, stiff-legged, jibbering madly.

They're still waiting for me, she thought. They know I can't . . .

A sob tore from her and she crumpled to the ground. It was over. The jackals were the proof. Newt and Derek were dead, they had to be, buried under the fallen rock.

And Lisa—how stupid had she been to believe that Lisa could still be alive?

Grief rolled over her more violently than the stone river. She finally understood how Derek could have waited silently at the bottom of the death trap, wanting only for his agony to be over.

"There is no peace that way, girl."

The chattering of the jackals stopped. Without even looking up, Jori reached out to rest her hand on Ragar's thick coat. "How do you always know when I need you?"

"I know." The wolf's rough tongue brushed her cheek. "But I also know that you would survive on your own, if you had to."

"But what if they're all dead? Lisa, Newt, Derek. My dad. How do I keep going then? Why would I even want to keep going?"

The wolf nuzzled her. "You simply do. For yourself. For the others that remain. For those who have not yet entered your life." Ragar gently pulled away, and Jori's arms slipped from her shoulder. "But stop using your mind for a moment, girl. What does your heart tell you? Do you truly believe you have lost them all?"

Jori hesitated, listened to something inside her. "No. It doesn't feel like they're gone. Not even Lisa."

"Then you still have hope, which brings with it all the strength you need. Now come, girl. We will find out what lies within the mountain."

Jori looked up hopefully. "We, Ragar?"

"Yes. This time, I won't leave you."

And Jori felt her strength returning.

★ ★ ★

Jori pulled herself to her feet and took a deep breath. Ragar nodded, and they picked their way cautiously around the base of the avalanche, to where the jeweled veins emerged once more from the fallen rock.

"If Newt and Derek are still alive," said Jori, "they'll know that I would have followed the threads. So they'll go that way, too."

"Perhaps. But if they believe they've lost you, they may have decided it was time to escape this place."

Jori hesitated, then heard a voice in her head—*We're not going to stop watching out for each other now.* She smiled briefly. "No. Newt wouldn't leave without trying to find me first. That's one thing I'm sure of."

They continued to follow the threads, and Jori scanned the towering dark peaks for a way to get inside. The Black Rivers looked even more hideous as they drew closer, thundering down toward the plain from gashes in the mountainside, hitting the parched earth with a loud hiss and an explosion of steam. The sides of the mountain glistened in the rising mist, looking more like skin than stone, and in places the membrane split apart, revealing a dull, white base that looked unsettlingly like bone.

Finally they came to a high, thick ridge that jutted out from the foot of the mountain. The strands streaked along its base and twisted around the far edge. From the other side came a low, dull moan, which swiftly rose to a howl of fury.

Ragar crouched low, and Jori flattened herself against the rock, which writhed grotesquely beneath her. She flinched, but then inched nervously toward the point where the threads disappeared. She forced herself to stop shaking, took a deep breath, and lunged around the edge.

A blast of cold air shrieked past her. Raising her eyes, she stared into the twisted face of Blood Mountain.

Its mouth gaped before her in a goblin's grin, stalactites dripping from its upper arch and thin spikes jutting from below. The inside of the cave glowed red, and Jori could see dozens of the twisted tapestry coils racing inside between the mountain's jagged teeth.

She forced herself to keep moving, tried not to think too much. But the mountain began howling again, alive and insane. Jori placed a trembling hand on Ragar's neck.

"Ragar, you told me once that you're my guardian. Wouldn't it be a good idea to talk me out of this?"

"Do you really want me to?"

Yes, Jori thought. Absolutely. "No. Of course not."

"Well, then." Ragar moved toward the mountain's open jaws, and Jori followed her into the cave.

They crept forward a few yards, then paused to let their eyes adjust to the dim light. Looking around, Jori saw that they stood in a massive cavern. It glowed dark red from the reflected light, oozed moisture like a raw abscess. It was so high that the ceiling was swallowed by darkness, so vast that a small village could have been built within it. In front of them, the floor of the cave rippled, dark and glistening, like a sea of frozen lava.

An odd scratching sound came from somewhere above them. Jori scanned the walls of the cavern and saw that they were scored with jagged grooves, as if a giant claw had scraped along the rock. The grooves created a series of ridges and pathways, along which Jori could see dozens of smaller openings—chambers or tunnels, she wasn't sure which.

A jackal slouched out from one of the openings, then another, then a dozen more. Jori flinched, but this time the creatures simply watched her, dark sentinels perched on turrets of stone.

"Are you ready?" asked the wolf.

Jori nodded. She forced her eyes back to the tapestry threads, which were snaking toward the far side of the cavern. There the cave narrowed abruptly, tightening like a throat. From this tunnel, the red light pulsed like a heartbeat.

"There, I guess," said Jori. The wolf nodded, and the two of them crossed the floor of the cavern under the mad eyes of the jackals. Their footsteps clicked and echoed, blending with the muffled roar of the Black Rivers that vibrated in the walls of the cave.

After what seemed like hours, but may only have been minutes, they reached the tunnel on the far side. The light continued to beat steadily, almost hypnotically, drawing them inside.

The passage was suffocatingly narrow, lined with rough columns that curved inward like scraped ribs. Behind the columns were heaps of stone that throbbed with every beat of the red light. And beyond the stones were more small caves, the same kinds of chambers that had spewed out the jackals in the larger cavern. Jori realized they were likely all connected, forming an elaborate warren inside the mountain.

"I hate this," Jori said. "What if they're just waiting to attack us here, where there's no place to run?"

A dry rustling came from her right. Ragar growled, and Jori backed away from the sound. She brushed against a pile of loose stones, sending an echo through the cave. The rustling came again, more frenzied this time, and her insides turned to water. Ragar lunged at her, shoving her violently forward. They raced through the tunnel and burst out the far side—into the most horrifying, most magnificent place Jori had ever seen.

Opening in front of her was another huge cavern, nearly twice the size of the first. But this one glowed with color, sparkled with the light of embedded crystals. The jeweled coil that had led Jori through the mountain now separated again into its dozens of shining strands. They flashed across the stone wall to a hundred different points around the cave, then floated out into the empty center, crossing over other each other and forming elaborate designs.

Giant white spiders crawled noiselessly among them.

Each of the creatures was several feet across. Silk flowed from their abdomens as they meticulously tended the strands—anchoring some, repairing others, and linking the tapestry threads with slender lines of their own. Spinning a huge, hideous, monstrously beautiful web.

Jori's eyes traveled down one strand, across another, lost in the intricate patterns. She realized suddenly that the colored threads all flowed in one direction—toward the center of the cave. There they met at a fragile cocoon that floated in midair, its perfect surface rippling with liquid rainbow colors that swirled like clouds. From it pulsed the strange red light.

"It's the heart," Jori murmured. "The heart of the tapestry." She looked at Ragar. "So it's where we have to go."

The wolf nodded. Jori saw a rough path leading from where they stood, down to the cavern floor. She and Ragar descended cautiously, watching to see how the spiders would react. But the creatures took no notice, intent on their tasks.

Finally they reached bottom and began to creep silently over the cold stone, careful to avoid the deadly strands that anchored the web to the ground. Jori heard a rustle and glanced up into the glistening canopy.

Newt hung above them, wrapped in a shroud of silken threads.

Jori gasped and Ragar snarled, ears flat against her head. Newt's eyes were closed, and a thin membrane of silk stretched across his open mouth. His arms were bound up against his chest, but the hands faced outwards, as though he'd been fighting to claw himself free.

"No," Jori wailed. "God, Newt, no . . ."

Suddenly Ragar leaped forward. "Wait!" she said. "Look at him!" Newt's chest was rising and falling, though only barely. "He's still alive!"

"But what can we do? He's up too high!" Jori looked around frantically, then spotted a cluster of stalagmites just a few feet away. She kicked at one, snapping it off. Lifting it over her head, she swung fiercely at the web.

The spike whipped through the sticky strands, which clung to its surface like glue. Jori leaned backward, pulling down with the weight of her entire body. The web began to stretch. Ragar darted directly underneath Newt.

"Harder, girl!" cried the wolf. And Jori gave one more powerful tug.

Ragar leaped into the air, her jaws locking onto the thick webbing near Newt's ankles. The strands of the web stretched even further, became thinner, and broke. The hideous bundle fell to the ground.

Frantic whispers echoed through the cave as dozens of legs skittered across the silk strands. Jori looked up in horror to see spiders converging on her. Then she heard a weak voice.

"Jori! Over here!"

Crawling out from a crevice in the wall was Derek, spider silk matting his hair and clothing. "Hurry! They stop when you get away from the web."

Jori grabbed Newt's shoulders, half lifting him, and staggered over to where Derek was struggling to his feet. The spiders stopped at the torn place in the web, working furiously to repair the damage.

Derek stumbled forward, helping Jori drag Newt the last few feet, into a small cavity in the rock. Together, they knelt beside him, ripping the strands from his body. But his face was gray, and his eyes remained closed. Derek put an ear to his chest.

"I don't know," he said miserably. "I can't tell."

"Come on, Newt," Jori pleaded. "Don't stop fighting now." She put her mouth over his and forced air deep into his lungs.

"Shit," said Derek, his face pale. "Shit, shit, shit. I kept going back and trying to get him down, but those things—"

Newt gasped. Convulsions wracked his thin frame and twisted his limbs, and his whole body slammed itself violently against the rock. Jori grabbed him to her, held him and rocked him, screamed out her fear as he strained against death.

Finally, the spasms weakened. His ragged breathing became more even, and his skin began to regain its color. His eyes flickered open—and widened as they fixed on Jori.

"Hey," he said weakly.

"Hey yourself," she said, tears finally flowing. "Don't scare me like that again, okay?"

"Okay," he whispered. "I won't, if you won't."

SEVENTEEN

THE GUARDIAN

Jori huddled with the boys in the damp stone shelter. She sat only inches from Newt, touching his arm occasionally to reassure herself that he really was alive.

He tried to sit up, then fell back exhausted. "Just a little longer," he said. "Then we can keep going."

"It's okay. You stay here and rest. I'll go on ahead."

"No. I just need a few more minutes and—"

"I can't." She was listening to the whisper of the web, picturing the throbbing cocoon at its center. "That thing out there is the key to all this. I know it."

"But the spiders . . ."

Derek interrupted. "If she doesn't touch the threads, they won't bother her. That's what happened to you. I saw you trip on a thread, and those things were all over you a second later. They didn't even notice me until I tried to get you down."

"So I'll be okay," said Jori. "Besides, Ragar—"

She stopped.

"What's wrong?" asked Newt.

"Ragar. She's not here."

"Who's not here?" asked Derek.

"The silver wolf. The one that helped me pull Newt from the web."

"I didn't see any wolf."

"She was there, right beside me. She said she wouldn't leave this time." Jori stared at a sliver of light that shone from the cave.

Newt pulled himself up on one elbow. "She hasn't left you. She's here, Jori."

"What?" Jori felt a rush of relief. "Where?"

He leaned over and touched her hand.

"Here." She stared at him, confused. "Haven't you figured it out yet? She's you, Jori. Just like Kieran was me."

She shook her head.

"No. That's crazy. Why would you even think that?"

"I told you once before. I've always known exactly who you are."

Jori began to protest, but Newt's face mirrored the certainty in his voice, the sureness of his belief. Trying to see herself through his eyes, Jori felt herself slowly open to the possibility. It would be so wonderful if Newt were right. But even if he weren't, he still saw Ragar when he looked at her. Maybe that was enough.

She nodded finally, then turned to Derek.

"Newt's going to be pretty weak for a while, so he's going to need your help. Wait with him for a while, and then the two of you follow me as fast as you can."

"Yeah, okay." Derek hesitated, seemed to be struggling with something. "Look. Just don't do anything as stupid as I probably would, okay?"

She bit back a smile. Then she eased herself out through the crack in the rock.

Once outside, she quickly scanned the cave. Where she had torn Newt from the web, only a single spider remained, carefully patting one last strand into place. The rest had returned to their endless checking, testing, repairing.

Her eyes fixed on the shimmering cocoon. She moved slowly across the stone floor, careful to avoid the glistening threads. As she drew closer, she heard an unexpected sound— the sound of someone singing. The gentle melody wrapped itself around her, warming her with achingly familiar words.

We're in the Moon Garden, the magic moon garden
Caressed by the silver-tipped leaves
Where the trees speak in whispers
And birds never sleep
And you see what you want to believe . . .

Jori cried out and raced toward the floating cocoon.

"Lisa!" screamed Jori, tears streaming down her face. "Lisa, it's me!"

The song stopped. Then she heard Lisa's bright, sweet voice.

"Jori?"

"Yes," Jori sobbed. "Oh God, Lisa, I've missed you so much. Mom's missed you so much."

"Why are you here, Jori?"

The question stung like a slap. Jori felt a twinge of fear.

"To find you, Lisa. To bring you home."

There was no reply.

"Lisa?"

"Come up here, Jori. I've missed you, too."

A delicate silk pathway spiraled down from the orb, stopping at Jori's feet.

She stepped onto it, then heard Newt yell from the other side of the cave.

"Jori, stop! Don't go up there!"

"I have to," she whispered, refusing even to look his way. She raced up the fragile pathway, her heart battering at her chest. When she reached the top, the wall of the thin globe melted away, then flowed back behind her.

The room was much larger than it had appeared, its curved walls smooth as pearl and blindingly bright. Jori shielded her eyes, then looked around her. The orb was divided into smaller areas by sheer, almost transparent curtains, all billowing gently though there was no breeze. Within each section were soft nests of silk—spaces to rest, to sleep, to dream.

In the center of the chamber was a low curving platform. On it stood a slim, brown-haired girl in long white robes. Lisa. Oh, God, it really was Lisa. She was facing away from Jori, her arms reaching toward an opening in the ceiling. Through this opening flowed the dream strands, drifting like sea grass above Lisa's head. Her hands brushed across them gracefully.

"Lisa? I'm here."

"Yes."

Jori ached to run to her, to throw her arms around her sister. But Lisa showed no emotion as her fingers danced over the gleaming threads.

"Lisa. Why won't you look at me?"

"Because you might not like what you see."

"What are you—"

Lisa spun toward her. Her eyes were covered with a thick white film, as smooth as glass and hard as scales. They locked Jori in a sightless stare.

"Oh, God," she whispered. "What happened to you?"

Her sister's smile was cold and lifeless. "Eyes aren't important if you live in a cave. And if you never intend to leave."

"What are you talking about?"

"This is my home now. Sight would just distract me from what I need to do."

Jori wanted to run from the once-sweet face that she loved so much, and that now frightened her so badly. But the dead eyes held her captive.

"He promised it to me, Jori. The old man. He said it would be mine."

"What would?"

"The tapestry. All of it, not just the part I dreamed. He said he needed someone to leave it to someday, someone who would care for it as much as he did. And Jori— he chose me." The white eyes gleamed.

"Then . . . why aren't you with him?"

"Because I'm the Guardian. I watch over the dreams, make sure that nothing in them hurts the tapestry."

Jori looked up to where the threads drifted into the chamber. As though feeling her gaze, Lisa reached up to caress them.

"All I have to do," she said, "is touch one of the strands. Then I can see the dream at the other end and know if it's still as beautiful as the tapestry deserves. Watch." Her fingers swept across a sapphire thread, and the orb immediately blazed into life. Images danced across the smooth walls and on each shimmering curtain. Images of an undersea king-dom with a trident-bearing king, and merfolk gliding among the coral.

Jori could see Lisa turning in a slow circle, the visions reflected on her blind eyes.

"Wonderful," sighed Lisa. "Still beautiful."

Jori felt her skin grow cold. "And when it's not?"

Lisa released the sapphire thread and drew out a thick black strand that writhed in her hand like a snake. "Then I send the Black River."

"So it was you," Jori said, her eyes on the squirming thread. "You sent the river to the desert palace."

Lisa's face darkened. "Yes. The dreamers there were poisoning it. I had to get them out."

"And then?"

"The River knows what to do with the ones it finds. It carries them into Maligor. Or lets the scavengers take them."

So Derek had been left behind for the Horridins. And Marisa . . .

This was a nightmare worse than the swamp hags, worse than the Horridins' pits. The thing in front of her wasn't Lisa anymore. It was something else—something as monstrous as the old man who had trapped them.

"But why do you want this, Lisa? Why is this better than coming home?"

The girl's white eyes went still.

"Do you really want to know?"

"Yes. Please."

Lisa reached into the strands once more, extracting one of pure spun gold. "He gave me another gift, the old man." Her voice became soft, seductive. "Take this and I can show you."

Jori stepped backwards. "No."

"I'm your sister, Jori. I wouldn't hurt you."

You wouldn't, thought Jori, if you were really Lisa. But maybe . . . maybe this is the only way to understand what's happened to you. She took a deep breath, closed her eyes, and grasped the thread.

A flash of heat ripped down her arm, jerking her off the ground and sucking her into a spinning tunnel of light. Panic tore through her. But before she could scream, the spinning stopped. A moment later, Jori heard a deep, warm, impossibly familiar voice.

"Hey, Jo! Get over here and give me a scroonch."

Her eyes snapped open. And there he was, grinning at her, arms spread wide and waiting to enfold her.

"Daddy?"

"Who were you expecting? The President?"

She stared at him, not moving.

"Well," he said. "If the mountain won't come to Mohammed . . ." He walked over and wrapped her in a suffocating bear hug, growling in mock ferocity. She melted against him, her anger at his leaving them vanishing in an instant. She felt the warmth of his body, smelled the odd mix of aftershave and chewing gum that always seemed to cling to him. He kissed the top of her head, and she held on to him desperately, her fingers clutching his shirt. Oh, how she'd missed his hug.

"Whoa, what's this?" he murmured. "Anything wrong, honey?"

"No," she said, her throat tight. "Nothing's wrong. It's just that . . . I've missed you."

"I was only gone two days, sweetie. I've had trips longer than that before." His voice took on a deeper note of concern. "You sure there's nothing wrong?"

Jori nodded, not trusting herself to answer.

"Well, that's good. Because I've got some great stories this time, but I told them I wasn't starting until you got home."

"Them?"

"Yes, them. You know." He sighed. "Have you forgotten their names *again?*"

Only then did Jori realize where she was. They were standing in the kitchen of their home, and it was almost dinnertime. Her mom was at the stove, scooping Rice-a-Roni into a bowl and cheerfully massacring show tunes. She stopped singing long enough to wave her spoon at Jori. "Nice to meet you," she said. "Sorry. Didn't catch the name."

Lisa was there, too, laughing as she helped to set the table. Officially, she was in charge of laying out the silverware, but at the moment she seemed to be more interested in tapping spoons on the table in time to her mother's songs. Jori felt a wild surge of relief. This was the Lisa she remembered. Always giggling, always chattering. Happiness spilling from her like a fountain.

And the really wonderful thing about the image in front of her was that she wasn't looking at a memory. This was a scene from now. Her mom's hair showed the threads of gray that had appeared during the past year, the textbooks on the kitchen counter were from the right grades, and Lisa was the age she should be.

But in this world, their dad was still with them. The accident had never happened.

"Okay," her father said, rubbing his hands together. "As we sit down to this wonderful dinner, only semi-burned tonight, who wants to hear why I had to eat grilled moose and fried prairie oysters for lunch the other day?"

"Well, at least it'll make the chicken taste better," said Jori's mom, depositing a platter of blackened poultry on the table. "Jori, honey, would you please get the glasses?"

Jori nodded and gave herself over to the dream. Turning toward the kitchen cabinets, she listened contentedly to her dad's voice, Lisa's giggles, and her mom's impassioned defense of the dinner. This is all I really need, she thought. Just the everyday stuff, with everyone and everything where it belongs. She lifted four glasses from the shelves. "Who needs ice?"

"I do, sweetie," said her mom.

"Me, too," said her dad. "And some water for me." Jori got the ice, filled her dad's glass from the faucet, and headed back toward the table. Lisa grinned at her, brown eyes sparkling. You see? her expression seemed to ask. Isn't *this* the way it should be?

Jori smiled, placing the glasses at each setting. And then she noticed that the scars were gone from her arm.

She stopped moving.

She looked at her family, complete once more, and her eyes filled with tears. Yes, this was how everything should be. But this was no longer how it was. Her mom wasn't making excuses for burned chicken. She was huddled alone in a silent house, praying for word of her lost daughters. And her dad . . . her dad wasn't sitting at the table, ready to tell her funny stories. Instead, he waited where she could visit him only until they closed the gates at dusk.

A sob swelled in her throat. She walked to where her father sat and gazed at him, trying to memorize every hair on his head, every wrinkle around his eyes.

"Daddy," she whispered. "Would you mind giving me another scroonch?"

He looked surprised. "Sorry, only one per day." But then he put his arms around her and squeezed. She breathed in his scent, felt for the last time the warmth of his arms, and hugged him until her arms began to ache.

And then she let him go.

"Okay, Lisa," she whispered. "I understand now. I do. But we can't stay."

Lisa looked at her in shock, and Jori vaguely heard her mother say something about not leaving the table before dinner was over.

"Come on, Lisa. We have to go."

"But why? Isn't this what you want, too?"

"Of course it is. But not if it means hurting Mom. Not if we have to throw away our real lives."

Lisa's eyes flashed, and the white scales slid over them again. "Shut up, Jori. Just . . . shut up. You had your chance before, and you blew it. You wrecked it." She motioned toward the table. "This is as real a life as I need. And if it's not what you want—" She stood up slowly. "Then get out."

"Not without you."

"Just try. Try, and see what happens."

Jori stepped toward her. Lisa shrieked and lashed out, striking Jori on the side of the head. Jori staggered, but grabbed her sister's arm before she could pull away. Then something clutched at her, seizing her like a giant hand, wrenching her out of her home, away from her parents. She cried out in anguish.

"Come on, Jori. Wake up!" She blinked. Newt was holding her, shaking her roughly. She was back in the cocoon. And the gossamer curtains billowed around her, empty of images.

"Are you okay? Are you back?"

"Yeah. Yeah, I'm okay. But Newt, Lisa's still in there."

"No, she isn't," said Derek.

He stood just a few feet away, one arm wrapped around Lisa's shoulders and his other hand clamped over her mouth. Lisa was snarling, trying to bite him, but he held on as stubbornly as a pit bull. Jori could see from his tight expression that he knew who had left him for the Horridins.

"We heard what she told you," said Newt, "and it didn't take a genius to figure out what dream you were headed for. I wasn't sure you'd come back."

She shook her head miserably. "I didn't want to. Not at all. But I knew where I was."

She heard a grunt and looked back toward her sister. Lisa's face was purple with rage, and she was kicking backward at Derek's legs.

Jori ripped two strips of cloth from the bottom of her shirt. "Sorry, Lisa." She gave one strip to Newt, who bound Lisa's hands behind her while Jori gagged her with the second strip.

"Come on," said Newt. "Let's get out of here."

He and Derek each grabbed one of Lisa's arms, forcing her to walk between them. With Jori in the lead, they moved clumsily down the spiral pathway, back to the floor of the cave.

All around them, spiders danced across the sparkling web. Lisa lunged forward, kicking wildly at one of the strands, but Newt and Derek yanked her back before she could reach it. She moaned in frustration, stopped struggling, and stumbled hopelessly between the two boys.

The journey across the cave seemed endless. They wove their way with painful slowness between the threads, staring at the shadows of the spiders who passed overhead. Newt turned pale, sweat beading on his forehead. But finally they reached the other side and climbed toward the opening of the tunnel.

Halfway up the path, Jori heard Newt yell. She looked back just as Lisa wrenched herself from the boys' grasp and leaped off the side of the ledge. Jori screamed, but Lisa landed in a net of dream strands just below where they stood. She fumbled behind her back, freeing her hands. Then she ripped the second strip from her mouth.

"They're getting away," she shrieked, picking her way across the strands as easily as any of the spiders. "Go after them!"

The creatures on the web froze, responding to the vibrations. Then they turned and began scuttling across the threads. Newt grabbed Jori's hand and dragged her into the tunnel.

"What about Lisa?" she cried, trying to pull away.

Newt yanked her around to face him. "It's too late. And if we don't get out now, your mom won't have anyone coming home to her."

Jori looked at him in shock. Then they raced madly through the tunnel, into the cavern where the jackals waited.

EIGHTEEN
FINAL BATTLE

The walls of the cavern glittered with eyes. The jackals perched on every rock, peered out from every crevice, like stone gargoyles on the spires of a church. But they were no longer alone. Horridins crept out of the caves to crouch next to them, their long talons clacking. Derek went rigid, pulling his torn arms close to his body.

"Shit," he whispered. "Shit, shit, shit."

Newt scanned the cave nervously. "So now what do we do?"

"They're not coming after us," Jori said, her own voice trembling. "They're just watching. Like when I came in. So I guess . . . I guess we just keep going."

They crept toward the center of the cavern. Derek's face had gone completely white, but the Horridins made no move to come after them.

Then the ground began to vibrate. From the mouth of the tunnel scuttled dozens of the white spiders, crawling up on the walls of the cave and blanketing the stone, a stark contrast to the dark creatures already waiting there. A moment later, a chamber high above the tunnel began to glow. Jori saw a shimmer of silk robes, and her sister glided onto the edge of the rock slab in front of it. Her sightless eyes gleamed in the shadows of the cave.

"You can't get away," she said, gesturing toward the watching army of monsters. "They won't let you."

"Lisa, no," pleaded Jori. "You can't do this."

"Oh yes, I can. And to protect this place, I will."

Grief ripped through Jori. Grief for her broken family, for her lost sister, and for Newt and Derek, who stood by her side. Both had survived unspeakable horrors, but might still lose their lives—victims of their loyalty to her, and the sick plotting of a twisted old man.

She felt a jagged bolt of rage.

"Lisa!" she cried, fury blasting away her sorrow. "Listen to me! *I won't let him hurt us anymore!*"

A chorus of vicious howls rang through the cave. Ragar streaked through the entrance, a dozen powerful gray wolves at her heels. They formed a bristling circle around Jori and the two boys, hackles raised and teeth bared.

Newt grabbed Jori's shoulder.

"See?" he said, staring at Ragar. "What did I tell you?"

Jori barely heard him. But the silver wolf, standing just next to her, seemed to double in size. Her eyes bored into the creatures that screeched and jibbered on the cliffs, and her growl shook the rocks of the cave. The jackals snarled in reply but slunk backwards; the spiders skittered higher on the walls.

"We will win this," Ragar said.

"I know."

Bursting through the ring of wolves, Jori raced toward the thing that had been Lisa. Ragar leaped after her, and the remaining wolves tightened their circle around Newt and Derek. Jori scrambled up a thin ribbon of stone, then clawed her way onto the ledge and stood in front of Lisa, staring into the girl's dead white eyes.

"This ends now," she said, her voice as hard as the rock they stood on. "If you want to do this to yourself, I can't stop you. But you're not going to take us with you."

The air behind Lisa shimmered.

"Jori," said a low, unexpected voice. "I'm disappointed in you." Her father stepped out of the darkness.

Jori stared at him, shock sweeping away her rage. How could he be here, outside the dream strand? But Lisa smiled with mad joy, stepping backwards to take his hand. "You see?" she said wildly. "You're the one who's wrong!"

"I expected more from you, Jori," their father said, his eyes showing his pain. "You weren't willing to make the sacrifice your sister did—not even if it could bring me back to you."

"No," whispered Jori. "That's not true."

"Then come with us. You saw what we can have." He held out his hand, and she could feel his love enveloping her. "We can all be happy again."

In a daze, Jori reached toward him. Then Ragar's jaws snapped in front of her face.

"Look at me, girl!" The wolf's eyes seared hers, and Jori blinked. "Now. See what he really is, not what he wants you to see."

Jori shivered, then raised her eyes once more. Standing behind Lisa, clutching her in his claws, was the warped old man of the tapestry.

"Lisa!" shrieked Jori. "Turn around! It's not Dad. God, Lisa, just turn around and look at him!"

Doubt flickered across Lisa's face. But then her white eyes gleamed more brightly, and she leaned back into the old man's embrace.

He grinned in triumph, stroking her hair.

"Don't do this," Jori begged. "It's not fair. She was just so unhappy when Dad died, and then . . . then I hurt her all over again. She doesn't know what she's doing."

"She knows," said the old man silkily. "She knows enough. You, on the other hand . . . You know far too much."

His right hand shot out, and lightning streaked from his gnarled fingers. The bolts struck Jori in the chest and she flew backwards, off the ledge and out over the cavern floor. She hung suspended in the air, clawing at nothing, her eyes wide with terror. The old man howled with delight as he made her spin and dance like a broken puppet.

Ragar tore down the stone pathway, shadowing Jori's movements, while Newt and Derek reached helplessly above them. The Horridins licked at the fear in the air, and the jackals barked in a blood frenzy.

With his other hand, the old man continued to stroke Lisa's hair.

"Another few moments," he said to her softly, "and we can return home. You'll never have to feel pain like this again."

Jori cried out in anguish, clinging to the last few seconds of her life. The old man was going to win after all. They'd be gone, all of them, and the only things that remained would be Lisa's twisted fantasy and the misery that would eventually kill their mother. She made one last, desperate attempt.

"Lisa," she sobbed. "Don't do this, please. I know Dad's gone, and I know how much I hurt you. But we've still got Mom, we're still a family, Lisa." Tears spilled down her face. "God, Lisa, please—don't destroy what we have left."

For a moment, Lisa remained motionless, the ghost of doubt sliding once more across her face. She pulled away slightly from the old man's embrace.

"You'd really hurt her?" she whispered.

"What, sweetheart?"

"Why would you hurt Jori?"

"Because, love, she treated you so badly."

Lisa turned slowly toward him. "But Dad would never hurt either one of us." And the scales fell from her eyes.

The old man roared and sank his claws into her shoulder. "It's too late," he hissed. He dropped his right hand.

The crackling nets that held Jori vanished. She plummeted toward the ground.

Lisa leaped forward, screaming Jori's name and thrusting out both hands. There was an explosion of light, a thunder of wings, and Angel burst into the cave.

He hovered briefly, eyes blazing, then dove toward the cavern floor. Swooping under Jori, he caught her on his powerful back. She clutched his neck and buried her face in the soft feathers between his wings.

Derek and Newt whooped in relief, jumping into the air and pounding each other on the back. A few moments later, Angel landed beside them and Jori leaped into their arms. From the ledge, she heard the old man's furious screams.

His face was now little more than a skull, red eyes burning from sunken sockets. He clutched at Lisa, who struggled against him, pale with horror. "You haven't won yet," he cried. "I still have her!"

Derek glared up at him. "Not for long," he muttered, and shot up the stone pathway.

"No!" cried Jori. "Derek, don't!"

He looked back, just for a moment. "I couldn't save Marisa," he said simply. Then he raced onto the ledge.

The old man hissed like a rabid rat.

"Get back," he snarled, his hands crawling onto Lisa's neck. "Get back now or—"

Derek sprang.

The old man collapsed as though his bones had shattered, but one hand still clawed for Lisa. She lurched away, then stumbled and began falling toward the ledge. Derek grabbed the edge of her robe, pulling her to safety.

"Run!" he yelled, and Lisa streaked down the tumbled rock. Jori ran to meet her, looking up at the ridge just as the old man struggled to his feet and slammed his cane into Derek. The boy crashed back into the rock and slid to the ground, unconscious. The old man struck him twice more, fury burning from his thin frame, then vanished into the darkness of the cave.

"Derek!" screamed Jori, staring at his broken body. Newt grabbed her arm.

"You and Lisa get out of here," he said. "I'll go after Derek."

"Newt—"

"Just go!"

Jori grabbed Lisa's hand and ran. Angel flew above them, and Ragar raced by their side, her wolves forming a living shield around them.

Now the old man's voice echoed through the cave, spurring the monsters with his fury. "Go after them! All of you! Destroy them now or you'll all perish!"

Jori heard a sudden roar, followed by the clatter of hundreds of legs and claws. Out of the corner of her eye, she could see the white bodies of the spiders scuttling across the wall, the jackals and Horridins blackening the floor beneath them.

She dragged Lisa to the mouth of the cave and they darted between the stone teeth. The wolves herded them across the barren ground into a withered field strewn with boulders. There they froze, open mouthed.

A host of wolves and unicorns thundered toward them, transforming the dark plain into a sea of white and gray. Ragar and Angel nuzzled the girls, then raced across the field to join their companions.

"Where did they come from?" Lisa whispered, staring at the magnificent army. But Jori, watching Ragar and Angel thunder side by side into battle, suddenly knew. She squeezed her sister's hand.

"From us."

The forces of Avendar reached the mountain just as the monsters spewed from its mouth. The two sides stopped and stared at each other, claws slashing at the air, hooves pawing the ground. Waiting for something.

Jori understood. She spotted a massive boulder and pulled Lisa toward it. They scrambled to the top, standing where the legions of light and dark could see them both.

Ragar and Angel looked toward them, wild-eyed, and Jori grabbed her sister's hand, raising their fists into the air.

"For Avendar!" she cried.

Ragar howled and Angel screamed a battle cry. They leaped toward the creatures of Maligor, and the two armies crashed together under the red light of the mountain.

The dark plain throbbed with hatred. The jackals slashed at their enemies' throats, while the ghostly white shapes of the unicorns rose and fell over the spiders, sharp hooves slicing through the creatures' legs, horns piercing the soft abdomens. Thick green fluid spurted from the wounds, and dozens of the spiders crumpled to the ground, jerking in violent death spasms.

Then the Horridins joined the battle, leaping onto the unicorns' backs, sinking sharp yellow teeth into their hides. The unicorns screamed in pain, and streams of blood cascaded down their white flanks. They speared the twisted creatures from each other's bodies, hurling them high into the air with their horns.

But it was the wolves who could not be stopped, the wolves who were everywhere. They attacked in a whirlwind of teeth and claws, clamping onto the jackals with vise-like jaws, bearing down until the bones broke. They pulled the Horridins from the backs of the unicorns, tore at their throats, ripped the skin from their bodies. Whenever one wolf went down, two appeared to take its place.

But the monsters kept coming, as deadly and relentless as the Black Rivers.

Jori screamed into the battle, sending all of her energy toward Ragar, toward her soul. Next to her, she could see Lisa's eyes fixed on Angel, her lips moving soundlessly. We can do this, Jori thought fiercely. However many of them come at us, we can beat them.

But then the mountain roared, and a crooked form materialized high above them. It was the old man, his arms outstretched in an obscene benediction, his body shaking in sick ecstasy.

"Did you really think you could win?" he cried. "That I'd let you destroy what has taken me lifetimes to create?" His hand swept downward, and Jori saw the crumpled bodies of Newt and Derek lying at his feet.

Cold fury filled her. "You bastard!" she screamed. "No one's going to destroy what *we* have, either!"

She turned to Lisa, saw her shaking with rage. Grabbing each other's hand once more, they stared up at the old man. White-hot power burned inside them, blazed from their skin, spun out into a column of light. And then it exploded, shrieking toward the raving creature on the mountainside.

A fireball of light engulfed the ridge. Ragar leaped from its hot center, and Angel materialized above her. The old man stumbled sideways in shock, tottering on the edge of the cliff. Angel screamed, striking out with his hooves, and Ragar lunged in from the side. Swinging at them wildly, the old man fell backwards onto the rock. The thin ledge crumbled beneath him, and he plummeted, howling, to the ground below.

As his body struck the stone, the mountain shrieked, fire exploding from every crevice. The creatures of the dark army froze, stunned. Then, broken and bloody, they began dragging themselves toward the shelter of the cave.

The black skin of the mountain burned and shriveled, revealing its white bone. Huge chalk-white chunks cracked off and tumbled down the sides, and the entire mountain began to crumble. The Horridins and jackals, cowering by the base, let out despairing howls as the rock crashed down around them. Then the whole mountain collapsed, sinking in on itself like a rotten corpse.

Minutes later, nothing remained but a steaming mass of red-hot rock, the stench of death, and the moans of the dying monsters within. Then the black waters that had once fed the rivers oozed up from the center of the rubble, drowning what remained alive.

The sudden quiet, the smoking ruins, were as eerie as the battle had been. And then, horrified, Jori realized that not only the monsters had been trapped when the mountain collapsed.

"No," she whispered. "Please, God, no."

The air vibrated beside her, bright and hot as a miniature star. She shielded her eyes until the glare softened. When she looked again, she saw Newt leaning unsteadily against Ragar, and Derek sliding weakly from Angel's back.

She sobbed and flung herself at Newt.

"You have *got* to stop doing stuff like that!"

"What were you worried about?" he said. "Think I was gonna screw things up now?"

Jori half laughed, half cried, then leaped at Derek and hugged him, too.

"Whoa," he said. "Must be another one of those sick, twisted nightmares."

Finally, Jori turned toward her sister. Lisa was trembling. She tried to speak, but then looked away, ashamed.

Jori threw her arms around Lisa's neck, pouring all of her love into the embrace.

"It's okay, Lisa. Everything's okay now." Lisa clung to her, sobbing.

Jori heard a gentle growl. She released Lisa, turned, and knelt, burying her face in Ragar's thick fur. "Thank you," she whispered. "Thanks for getting me through this." The wolf crooned softly and licked Jori's cheek. Next to them, Lisa rested her cheek against Angel's face, gently stroking his neck.

"I thought I had failed you," he murmured.

She shook her head. "I was the one who sent you away. Even though you were the best part of me."

Derek cleared his throat. "So, okay," he said, folding his arms. "This is really touching. But do you think maybe now we can just get the hell out of here?" As the others laughed, he smoothed back his hair and swaggered over to Lisa. "By the way, I'm Derek. The guy who saved your life."

"Hi, Derek," said Lisa shyly, her face turning as red as Jori's hair. "And thanks." Derek grinned. Then he turned, raised an eyebrow at Newt, and nodded toward Jori.

What's this? Jori thought. But Newt walked over and took her hand, lifting her up from where she still knelt next to Ragar.

"Hugging a wolf is okay," he said. "But maybe I've got a better idea." He kissed her then, quickly and sweetly. When he lifted his head, they were both smiling.

"Wow," he said. "Scariest thing I've done since I got here."

Jori laughed softly, then leaned toward him. But no, she thought reluctantly, this would have to wait. She squeezed Newt's hand, then turned to Lisa. "Ready to go home?"

Lisa's eyes sparkled. "As soon as we can."

"Allow me to help with that part," Angel said, walking over to them and spreading his wings. "Hop on."

For the last time, Jori climbed onto Angel's strong back. She looked again at the ruins of the mountain, and at the band of unicorns and wolves who stood watching them.

"Thanks," she whispered. "Thanks, all of you."

For a moment there was silence. Then one of the wolves began to howl. The rest joined in, and the unicorns added their chorus of high, musical voices. The strange cry followed them as Angel launched himself into the air and began to beat his glorious wings. But there was one voice Jori hadn't heard.

"Ragar!" she cried, twisting to look at the dark plain beneath them. Then she smiled as she saw the wolf, a silver blur, keeping pace with Angel as he flew them back toward Avendar.

The journey back was as swift and sweet as dreams were supposed to be. Below them, the tapestry shimmered, a brilliant patchwork of color and light.

Jori watched the gleaming landscapes unfurl. But then she grew still, realizing that more than the tapestry was on display below her. She was also seeing the fates of its victims in what was left of their dreams.

Some, like the desert kingdom, were deathly still and fading to gray—frozen in the moment of time where they had twisted into nightmares. Others were nearly erased by the waters of the Black Rivers. But, perhaps most frightening of all, some remained vividly colored, vibrant with life.

The others had now stopped talking as well.

"What about the ones who are still there?" Newt asked quietly. "What happens to them?"

But Jori couldn't bear to think about the answer.

NINETEEN

ONE LAST DREAM

Jori woke in the tapestry room of the old man's house, holding tightly to Lisa's hand. She saw the boys stirring as well, each grasping a segment of Jori's dream strand. Around them, the other dreamers still slept, their soft breathing the only sound, the faint rise and fall of their chests the only movement. Jori felt Lisa gently pull her hand away, then watched as her sister stared at the still forms. A moment later, Lisa turned and moved silently toward the door. Jori herself remained motionless, and Newt looked at her, questioningly.

"You go ahead," she said. "I just need a little more time."

Newt nodded, and she listened as he, Derek, and Lisa descended the stairs. A few minutes later she followed them, walking through the doorway of the crumbling house and into the frigid air of the dead garden. One by one, she and the others turned to stare at the faint glow in the second floor window. Lisa was the first to look away.

"Let's go home, Jori," she said. "I want to see Mom."

Jori felt a burst of pure happiness, imagining the screams that would erupt when their mom opened the front door and saw them. She nodded, and they all headed toward the broken garden gate. Derek quickly positioned himself next to Lisa, and the two walked slightly ahead, heads bent toward each other. Jori smiled.

She felt a cold nose touch her hand.

"Hey, Gopher," she said, turning and bending down to him, "I'm glad you waited. You ready to come home, too?" She scratched behind his ears, and he sighed contentedly.

Newt crouched next to her. "Okay," he said. "Now tell me why you hung back in the tapestry room just now."

Jori hesitated, then tugged at the pocket of her jacket. Two long legs poked out the top, then jerked back inside.

"I scraped up some of the crystals, too. I can't just leave them trapped there, Newt."

"I didn't figure you could." He looked at her affectionately. "So when are we going to do this, crazy girl?"

He said *we*, she thought, smiling. "As soon as we know who we're looking for, I guess. And as soon as I can figure out how to make my mom understand."

"She'll understand," he said. "If she's anything like you."

Jori nodded, then glanced toward the alley. "Come on," she said, taking his hand. "We'd better catch up. I'm not sure I trust Derek with my sister." Newt laughed, and they hurried after the others. But Jori's thoughts soon drifted back to the tapestry, to the dreamers still lost in its gleaming strands.

We'll find you, she promised them. We'll find you, and we'll bring you home.

THE END

About the Author

Bonnie Dobkin grew up in and around Chicago. She was a frighteningly ordinary and hideously well-behaved child. To compensate, she now tries to escape normalcy through writing, by acting in musical theater, and, once, by being on a reality show. When in adult mode, Bonnie is the editorial director for language arts for an educational publisher, the mother of three semi-grown sons, wife to a Vegas-obsessed dentist, and the love object of a ninety-pound mutt of dubious heritage. *Dream Spinner* is her first novel. Visit Bonnie Dobkin on the Web at www.bonniedobkin.com